THE MAGICAL PRISON OF MIDDLE PARK

THE NEW KENT CHRONICLES: BOOK TWO

MIKE JONES

The Magical Prison of Middle Park
The New Kent Chronicles: Book Two
by
Mike Jones

LAMPPOSTS ATTACK

Sammy, a twelve-year-old middle school boy with fair skin, brown eyes, and tousled brown hair, wrapped the harness around his puppy's little body. "Hey, Jane. I'm going to take Elizabeth for a walk in the park." He turned the doorknob.

Jane stuck her head out from behind the computer monitor. "Okay, Sammy. Just be back by six. Bob is making chili." She turned back to her screen.

Sammy flew out the door and down the apartment stairs. He and Elizabeth reached the park in no time. They entered at Eighty-Sixth Street and took the winding path toward the skating rink.

Sammy Nichols fed Elizabeth Bennet a bacon treat. "You like the park? Yes, you do because you're a good girl! And you walk so nice, like a good puppy. Come on, let's go a little more, okay?"

The eight-month-old female Yorkshire Terrier puppy excitedly looked up at Sammy then jumped playfully, catching his hand with her sharp teeth.

"No jumping, Elizabeth. We're learning to walk with the

leash, remember?" Sammy knew she remembered, but it could be difficult for a puppy to curb her excitement.

Elizabeth let out a squeaky bark. The park was their favorite place to walk. Sammy enjoyed the tranquility of the trees and open spaces. Elizabeth seemed to enjoy the smell of the grass and rolled in it often. Middle Park was well-traveled by many people and animals. Sammy assumed that was why Elizabeth enjoyed it so much. There was always something new to sniff out.

"No rolling in deer poop today, okay? You know, it looks like this is going to be our year, like things are beginning to look up for us. I was so excited when Bob and Jane brought you home. They're nice people. I've lived with other foster parents before, but none of them were ever as nice as Bob and Jane." Sammy allowed Elizabeth to sniff at the foot of a giant spruce tree.

"None of my previous foster parents ever bought me a dog. Some of them were mean too. The Marconis even tried to take my runes from me. They said the runes might be valuable, that they wanted to see how much they could get for them at the swap meet, and if I was going to be part of the family, I had to 'do my part.'"

Sammy ran his finger along the braided leather bracelet that held two metal charms. "I'm glad I hid them. I was afraid I'd lose them, but I'd rather lose them than have the Marconis sell them. We're lucky this park is so big. I buried them deep in the nature preserve, and they were still there when I dug them up last month."

They strolled down a deserted path. "I knew exactly which one was for you—the Wynn rune. I simply had a feeling that you were supposed to wear the Wynn. And I wasn't afraid that Bob and Jane were going to sell them on me. They even drove me to the library and checked out a book on runes so I'd know what they meant. That's how I knew that the Wynn was for you, 'cause you're a happy dog, and you make me happy. Elizabeth, you're a true friend.

"I've never really had a friend before. The other kids in the group homes weren't really friends. They were just the kids I lived with. At first, I thought they were nice, but I realized that just because you spend time with someone, doesn't make them a friend. A friend is someone who gives you the last cookie. They always took my cookies."

Sammy bent down to untangle Elizabeth's leash. He unwrapped the puppy and straightened her harness, admiring the Wynn rune that hung there along with her dog tags. It glimmered in the sunshine.

"Did you clean your rune? It's so shiny. Did Bob or Jane polish it for you?"

Sammy thought it strange that the rune sparkled so much. He remembered her rune to be a dull pewter type of metal, but today, it sparkled like highly polished jewelry.

A glint caught Sammy's eye. He looked down at his own wrist. His two runes also shimmered like new.

"Elizabeth? My runes changed color too. How'd that happen? I never take them off, and I didn't polish them. Did they polish themselves? I probably just imagined that they were dull before. Who knows, maybe the time they spent in the ground did something to them, like a reverse patina. It could just be the bright spring sunshine."

Sammy shrugged. "Whatever. Come on, let's get going. You know we need to walk, or you'll have too much energy at home. I don't want you running in circles when I'm trying to do my chemistry homework. It's getting late too."

They proceeded to stroll through the park's many lanes, over bridges, and through tunnels. Middle Park was a maze of winding paths. One could wander for days through its various lanes and never take the same route twice.

Elizabeth stopped dead in her tracks.

"What? Why are you stopping? Are you afraid of the lampposts? We've passed about a hundred already. What makes these special?"

Sammy and Elizabeth came upon two black lampposts on either side of the path at the top of a lonely hill.

Elizabeth planted herself on the pavement and refused to move. Sammy thought about dragging her, then thought better of it. She was so small, only five pounds or so. He could easily pull her up and make her walk, but he didn't like the idea of forcing his one and only friend into doing something she didn't want to do.

"Come on. They're only light poles like the ones in front of our building. They're not going to hurt you. What if I pick you up? Is that okay?" Sammy bent down and scooped her up into his arms. He cradled her in one arm like a football, bringing his face close to hers. She smelled of oatmeal shampoo.

"It's okay. We're not scared." Sammy carried her past the lampposts.

Elizabeth yelped and howled like she'd never done before.

2

INTRUDERS

The heavy iron door slammed shut with a deafening thud. The familiar boom reverberated through the tunnel.

So this one's the entrance today? Which will it be tomorrow?

Bart removed a small brown leather-bound book from the breast pocket of his shabby brown jacket and noted the location of the door.

"Tricky, tricky. You're still playing tricks, even after all these years. I'll learn your secrets, you wait."

If there's a pattern, I'll find it. I've been working at it long enough.

Bart looked left, then right, hoping no one had seen him exit through the heavy metal door. As usual, no one had. Once again, he only saw his familiar tunnel lined with so many doors.

He turned to the right and walked slowly, counting his steps as he walked, noting the paces as he passed each door.

Twenty paces to the mead hall, thirty to the pagoda. It's changing quicker now and more randomly than before. It's toying with me.

"He's toying with me."

Bart reached the end of the tunnel. The bright sunlight burned his sensitive eyes. "I've got to get out more often, or these old eyes will be useless."

They've aged so much faster than the rest of me. I've kept most of my youth, but at what cost? Sure, I might look like the young person I was so long ago... this blasted place will be the death of me, piece by little piece.

The sunshine warmed his pale, cool skin, and the chill in his bones was fading.

He heard voices, sending him into high alert.

Who the blast was that?

The hills surrounding the tunnel usually blocked most noise, and not many people came very close to the tunnel. Anonymity was part of its charm.

He gathered his wits and snuck farther from the tunnel's opening, feeling somewhat shy of the outside world. He didn't venture out very often, but this was one of the times he had no choice. If someone was able to get so close without being turned away, there were sure to be problems close behind.

The lampposts. They'll never get past the lampposts.

Bart crept out into the open, over the slight rolling hills that surrounded the tunnel. The bright sun shone on his shabby and tattered old brown suit. It looked more like rags than a finely tailored suit fit for a gentleman.

He crested the last hill, and the lampposts came into view. He saw a young man, slightly thin to average build, 160 to 170 centimeters tall, shaggy brown hair, with no obvious signs of the Craft about him. The young man held a small dog.

They walked through the Jacob's Ladder. The electricity leapt from its source at the lampposts and latched onto the dog. Except for the dog's brief fright, the two barely noticed the traveling arch of high-voltage electricity. It finally released its grip once the boy and dog had cleared the posts.

That damned Tesla and his rubbish security devices! How am I supposed to do my job as caretaker when his bloody machines refuse to work?

Bart scurried behind an old hemlock and spied on the curious boy and his puppy. The dog strained toward the tunnel.

The arch lightning's intact. How did they pass through a hundred-thousand-ampere arch unharmed?

The blue electricity climbed up the lampposts as usual. Tesla's security gate appeared to be in normal working order. The dog did not look normal. It wore the unmistakable brilliant-blue aura.

Who are they? And since when do dogs have the Aura of Ether? They must be up to no good.

The sky opened up, and the rain crashed down, but Bart hardly noticed.

Something's wrong.

"Very wrong."

3

THE PUPPY THIEF

Sammy fretted. He hated to hear Elizabeth cry in pain. "What? What's going on?" He put her down on the ground after clearing the posts. "You okay?" Sammy looked around for German shepherds. She was afraid of shepherds, but there were none; the area was deserted.

Elizabeth smiled at Sammy and barked playfully.

"You can't scare me like that. I thought you hurt your leg again." Sammy got down on one knee and examined Elizabeth from head to toe, making sure all her parts were in good working order. After poking and prodding her and not seeing any sign of pain, they continued on their walk, far from the park's more populated areas.

"Are we lost? Have we been here before?" Sammy stopped and looked back behind him. "This looks like our usual path, but something's different. I don't remember all of those doors in that dark tunnel over that hill."

Why not check it out? We've got nothing better to do.

Elizabeth jerked and strained like an Alaskan sled dog,

seemingly determined to continue on their current path. She nearly yanked Sammy's arm from its socket.

"Ouch. Stop pulling. I thought you were leash-trained already." Sammy took a plastic Tupperware container from his pocket and grabbed a bacon treat from it. He showed the treat to Elizabeth. "You get a treat when you heel, remember?"

To his surprise, Elizabeth was not interested in the treat at all. "You don't want it?"

She jerked at the leash in response.

"Elizabeth, stop. You're all excited. Chill out." She didn't chill. She pulled harder.

The sky opened up, and a torrential monsoon assaulted them. "C'mon, let's go home. It's pouring."

The dog continued to yank onward, oblivious of the storm. Usually, she would have been frightened by the loud, booming thunder, but not that day. Instead, she strained like a mini sled dog determined to cross the frozen tundra. The new one-inch nylon leash tore in two, and Elizabeth shot off like a dart.

"Hey, come back." Amazed that the tiny five-pound dog was able to break the nylon leash, Sammy ran after her, chasing her up the hill. But she was faster than him. Sammy panicked. In an instant, he broke out in a drenching sweat. He could barely catch his breath.

Elizabeth was brave but foolish. She had no idea how fragile and vulnerable she was out in the open. Without his protection, anything could have happened. She could be attacked by a rabid animal, or a bird could swoop down and carry her off. She could get hit by a bus.

Sammy, chill out. There're no buses in Middle Park. Breathe.

The dog finally stopped at the top of the hill. Her head and eyes were fixed on the tunnel below. She held one paw up, ready to take that next lightning-fast step. Sammy ran up behind her, hoping to snatch her up before she took off again. He reached for her and felt her soft, straight hair on the tips of his fingers, but she slipped away just before he was able to get a grasp on her little body. She ran down the other side of the hill, straight for the tunnel under the bridge... the tunnel with the doors.

He followed as she disappeared into the dimly lit tunnel. Sammy stopped at the tunnel's entrance. He bent over, out of breath, and rested his hands on his knees. She was twenty or thirty feet inside the tunnel. She was eating something.

"Elizabeth, no! I told you not to eat garbage from the ground."

She paid him no mind. Sammy took a closer look and was shocked at what he saw. The tunnel was lined with strange doors on either side. They looked totally out of place, as if they were brought there from somewhere else. Some were modern clear glass like those in one of the downtown high-rises. Some were made of ancient-looking wood and reminded him of an illustration in the old *Hansel and Gretel* picture book at the library.

Even stranger, Elizabeth was eating from a sparkling white dinner plate. It sat on the cobblestone pavement, directly in front of a prison cell door that looked like one in the old *Count of Monte Cristo* movie.

What the... steak frites?

She gobbled down French fries as if it was her last meal. She held the steak down with her two front paws, ferociously gnawing at it, desperately trying to tear off a piece of meat small enough to fit in her tiny mouth.

"Oh no. Elizabeth, stop!" Sammy feared the worst. He had heard of terrible people leaving out tainted food for poor, hungry animals.

He ran toward the dog, hoping she hadn't eaten enough to make her ill, while calculating the time it would take to carry her out of the park and down to the animal hospital on Sixty-First and Second. He finally reached her and snatched her up, kicking away the white plate of steak frites. The plate shattered against the metal, and the steak flew through through the bars to the other side of a shadowy dark cell. Elizabeth writhed and squirmed to free herself from Sammy's arms.

Desperately holding on to the tiny writhing puppy, Sammy was amazed he still held the broken leash. Kneeling down, he placed Elizabeth on the cobblestones, hoping to tie the leash to her harness just in case she wiggled free from his hold.

As he bent to gently place her down on the cobblestones, she leapt from his arms, yelping out a shrill cry as her feet hit the pavement. She hopped back to the cell door and the irresistible steak.

"Oh no." Sammy hated to hear her cry in pain. Hoping she hadn't injured a leg, he ran back toward her and the cell door.

She scratched and pawed at the cell door, trying to squeeze her small body through the metal bars, determined to get to the suspicious steak.

Sammy hurried, relieved that the dog didn't seem to have a broken leg and couldn't get through the bars.

To Sammy's astonishment, a pair of bone-white hands seemingly passed through the solid metal bars. They clasped around Elizabeth's small frame and pulled her though as if they weren't even there. She writhed and bit at the hand Then she was gone.

Sammy reached the cell door and caught a last glimpse of a hooded figure carrying Elizabeth Bennett out of sight.

"Hey!" Sammy screamed. "Stop! Elizabeth!"

The figure in the dark hooded robe was gone, having disappeared into the shadows beyond the cell door. The dim light in the tunnel didn't reach far through the cell door, and Sammy couldn't see farther than a few feet past the bars.

Sammy wrapped his hands around the dirty, cold bars and pulled. He strained and yanked, and for a moment, he actually imagined he might be strong enough to bend the bars. But he wasn't. The bars didn't move. They only taunted him with their silence. He'd never wanted superhuman strength before, but at that moment, a Ring of Ogreish Might would have been perfect.

Sammy flew into a panic. He rubbed the sides of his head as if somehow he could massage his mind into discovering the solution to how to get through the cell door. He paced back and forth, muttering. How had he lost his only friend?

This can't be happening. He searched for a back door, dashing out of the tunnel and scrambling up the side of the hill. Sammy crossed the footpath laid over the hilltop, slid down the opposite side of the hill, and ran back into the tunnel, completing a circuit. "It doesn't make sense!"

After a torturous minute of heart-throbbing anxiety, Sammy came to his senses. He thought about calling the police or the FBI. *They'll help, they have keys and resources. They have SWAT and K-9 units. They'll track down Elizabeth and arrest her abductor.*

He thought about calling his foster parents but decided against it. He didn't want them to think they'd adopted a troublemaker.

He reached into his pocket, pulled out his phone, and frantically dialed 911.

"911," a woman's droning, robotic voice said. "What's your

emergency?"

"Hello? Send the police, quick. They stole Elizabeth."

"Who stole Elizabeth?" asked the operator.

"I don't know who. There was a plate and a steak, and a guy grabbed her through the bars. And there's evidence. Send the CSI."

"Where are you, sir?"

"I'm in Middle Park."

"Where in Middle Park, sir? We need your exact location to send a unit."

"I don't know where. The path kept changing on me. I came in by the museum and walked on the gravel path for a few minutes. I'm by the lampposts."

The woman snorted. "You're by the lampposts?"

Sammy paced back and forth. "You have to hurry. They're getting away."

The phone line crackled. "Sir, we need to know where you are so we can send someone to help."

Sammy's voice squeaked. "Hurry. Use my cell signal to triangulate my location? You're the government. You know this stuff."

She grunted. "Sir, we're doing our best. Now, calm down and retrace your steps. How did you get to your current location?"

"Listen, I entered the park at the Natural History Museum. I took the paved path past the skating rink. I made a left at the rowboats. When I got to the old castle, I took the gravel path toward the amphitheater, but then I made a left on a dirt path over the hills... I think."

The operator's tone perked up. She actually sounded interested. "Over the hills? Sir, we're sending units to your location now. Don't go anywhere. Stay in one place. What's your name?"

Sammy breathed a sigh of relief. "Sammy Nichols."

Sammy heard the scratching sound of pencil on paper. "Elizabeth Nichols, got it."

Sammy shook his head. "No. She's Elizabeth Bennett."

The operator cleared her throat. "I'm putting all this into the alert system. We need to know exactly what she looks like and what she's wearing."

He ran a hand through his unkempt locks. "Her hair is blue and tan. She was wearing a black harness. She's five pounds."

The operator groaned. "Sir, is Elizabeth your sister?"

He palm-slapped his forehead. "No, she's my dog. Just hurry."

The operator spoke to another person, but Sammy couldn't make out what she said. She then blurted rather loudly into the phone, "Animal control will be dispatched to your area. Stay at your location. Their average arrival time is between two and three hours. Dial 911 if you need further assistance." The operator hung up on him.

Sammy slammed the flip phone shut. "What the freak? She hung up on me!"

"Did you call 911?" a gruff voice demanded from behind him.

Sammy jumped out of his skin. He turned and saw the disheveled, middle-aged cop staring at him. His uniform was so faded, it looked purple. An old silver revolver was in a holster that hung low around his hips like a cowboy.

He noticed a different patch on the cop's arm. "You're not a city cop."

The cop mumbled under his breath. "I'm Park Police. You lose a dog?"

Sammy had been through Middle Park many times

before, and he'd never come across a park cop. *This guy's a cop?*

Sammy pointed to the cell door. "She was kidnapped, in there."

The cop adjusted his gun belt, resting his hand on the rusty revolver. "That didn't happen. You can't call 911 for fun. It's a crime to prank the emergency line. If you want to have fun, why don't you go to the courts and play ball like a normal kid?"

Sammy's mouth fell open. He tried to calm himself and focused on talking slower. Cops didn't like when kids got excited. "It did happen. There was a steak. She was eating the steak, and then someone grabbed her through the bars."

The cop chuckled. "Kid, there's nothing behind the doors. It's an installation by the art college. They're not real."

Sammy pointed to the white ceramic shards at their feet. "I know what happened. Someone stole my dog from behind that door. Look, the plate is still on the ground."

The cop's phony smile faded from his face. He took Sammy by the arm and led him out of the tunnel to a golf cart parked at the tunnel's entrance. The cop's large, pale hand guided Sammy into the golf cart. "Sit here."

Sammy sat as the pale man loomed over him.

The park cop took a pencil and notebook from his shirt pocket. "What's your name?"

This wasn't going how Sammy had hoped. This guy wasn't the FBI or the National Guard. He wasn't going to help. Sammy stood, reached into his pocket, pulled out his phone, and dialed 911.

If he's not going to help, I'll find someone who will.

The cop snatched the phone from Sammy's hand. "Kid, look. There's no dog and no door."

Sammy reached for the phone. "Give me my phone

back."

The cop wasn't having it. With his free hand, he grabbed Sammy's arm. The man's large fingers bit into Sammy's wrist and squeezed, twisting it in ways it wasn't supposed to move.

Pain shot through his arm, taking his breath away. Sammy fell to one knee. "Ahhhh. Okay, okay."

The cop released him.

Sammy stood, rubbing his wrist. The pressure of the cop's grip had left four distinct red finger marks.

The cop pointed a finger directly at Sammy's face, only millimeters from his nose. Sammy could see only the finger. It was gross and dirty with black lines in the cracked, pale skin. Dried blood was in the area where the nail should have been. It had been clearly chewed away. The finger trembled. "Kid, there's no dog. There's no tunnel and no doors. We're going down to the station. Child Protection Services needs to talk to you after we get you checked out."

Sammy looked away, disgusted by the horrid finger.

The cop grabbed Sammy by the cheeks. "Look at me when I'm talking to you."

Afraid to look into the cop's pale blue eyes, Sammy fixated on the man's wrist. It had a faded indigo tattoo in the shape of the letter F. He'd seen that F before. It was one of the runes in his book.

What's up with that tattoo?

This wasn't how things were supposed to go. Everything was going so well up until today. "I'm sorry. I'll behave." He didn't know what else to say.

The cop released Sammy's cheeks. He pulled a set of silver metal handcuffs from his belt. He twirled them around on his filthy finger and showed them to Sammy. "You don't want to wear these bracelets."

Sammy sat back in the seat, defeated. Having been through the system, he had seen this kind of thing happen a dozen times. He knew what came next. They would check him into the hospital for a few days to be evaluated until they could make sure he wasn't a danger to anyone. Then he would go to Juvenile Detention, and finally, back to the group home. He would probably never see Elizabeth, Bob, or Jane again.

It was good while it lasted.

The cop shoved the notebook back into his shirt pocket and shook his head. "Look, kid. Sometimes you gotta know when you're beat. You can get another dog, but you can't get another life. You understand me? She's ours, and we're on a time limit here. I ain't gonna let some punk kid like you stand in our way. I had enough of these goody-two-shoes making all the rules, telling me what I can't do. We're bringing Durga back, and he'll restore the Herrenvolk to our full glory."

The hair on Sammy's neck stood on end. He leapt from the golf cart and fled at full speed, never looking back. He wasn't going to let that nut-bag catch him. That dumpy cop stole Elizabeth for sure. He ran over the rolling hills as far as he could.

He thought about running home to Bob and Jane but changed his mind. They didn't have any experience with this kind of thing. They didn't know what it was like. They wouldn't be able to help.

That fat old cop wasn't going to catch Sammy in his little go-cart. It wasn't built for speed or forest areas. Sammy made for the nature preserve. The cops wouldn't find him in there.

They're probably too chicken to even try.

4

THE BUTCHER ON HIGH STREET

Bart was surrounded, backed up against a brick wall on High Street. The butcher and his two sons flanked him on either side.

"Sir, I really don't want to cause any trouble," thirteen-year-old Bart said. "I'll just be on my way, and we'll forget this whole misunderstanding ever happened." He looked the burliest of the three assailants in the eye. "I wouldn't want you three gentlemen to have any problems with the coppers."

"Coppers? You thieving street scum, you gonna stand there and threaten me with my wife's Sunday meat pie in your hand? You got some nerve." The barrel-chested butcher waved his cleaver inches from Bart's nose. A coal man watched from across the street.

The butcher didn't take kindly to prying eyes and shot the man a glare. "And what are you staring at?"

The coal man gave his pony a tap. "We'll just be on our way then. Come on, Betsy." Bart's only hope of intervention trotted off.

A miniature redheaded version of the butcher pointed

his red-stained finger. "That's the one, Father, the one I been telling you about. He been robbing and stealing for months. Come by after the frost, all manner of good turn up missing since he been round."

Bart stepped back on his right foot, ready to bolt. "Surely, you'll listen to reason, sir. I can explain. Nothing here but a misinterpretation of the facts. We can work this all out in a mutually beneficial manner. No need for brutality."

The younger of the butcher's two ginger-haired boys pointed. "There. Look, Dad, on his feet. Tommy Boyle's new lace-ups if I ever seen 'em. Tommy's mum were squiring away every spare coin she got her hands on, going on two year now. She finally take Tommy down to Connor the Cobbler, Tuesday last. Next day, boots gone missing, right from under Tommy's bed while he sleep, dead of night."

Bart grasped at straws. "Sir, I can assure you, these boots are my own, given by the good father down at Saint Michael's only yesterday. You see, my previous ones were in a frightful state of disrepair, and the father took pity on me. If you would accompany me, the father will surely testify to my innocence and bear witness."

The butcher grabbed Bart by the collar of his oversized shirt, the cleaver resting on Bart's ear. "You little thief, you gonna drudge Father Maloney's good name through this here? You gonna dirty a good man with your evils?"

In a flash, Bart slipped out of his oversized dingy grayed pullover and sped off too fast for the butchers to react. He ran through the street at full speed, knocking over several petticoat-clad ladies who were window-shopping at the haberdashery.

"Begging your pardon, my lady," shrieked the butcher, only steps behind.

Bart caught the reflection of his own grime-streaked

cheeks and emaciated torso in a shop window. His collarbone and ribs protruded through his chest. This life wasn't for him. It was no way to live. He broke left into an alley, out the other end, then right down Parson's Street. *I'll lose them on the roof. Fallon won't appreciate guests.*

He sprinted the two blocks, his boney chest heaving and burning. He was almost there. Finally, he reached the tenement building, ran through the front door and up the stairs to the roof. The butcher's screams of rage echoed through the hall. It was a long jump to the adjacent roof. Bart made the landing but lost his breath on impact. His cracked rib hadn't healed yet.

The butcher screamed from across the gap. "Get back here, street rat!"

Fighting through the pain, Bart found the door to the stairs and bounded down to the first floor. He reached the safety of apartment one. The door was unlocked. He barged in, latching the bolt behind him.

The apartment was empty except for the broken mirror on the wall. "Fallon! Fallon! Where are you?" Fallon was gone. It was all gone, everything he'd worked for over the last two months. Fallon had made off with the whole of their loot. The butcher's booming footfalls echoed through the hall. The doorknob jiggled, and the rotted wooden door trembled and bowed under the pressure of the butcher's weight. Dust fell from what was left of the crumbling ceiling.

Bart tried the windows. They were nailed shut, evidence of Fallon's paranoid security measures. He was trapped. He hid in the closet. The apartment door flew from its hinges and crashed against the mottled floorboards. He peered through the crack between the door and its frame.

The butcher pointed his stained cleaver at the closet,

and his two boys grinned ear to ear. "Come out, little street rat. We've got something for you. Don't be afraid. I won't break all your bones. You got enough to spare though. I saw 'em all, you without your shirt. You ain't had a proper meal, have you? That's all right. I'll leave my missus' pie when I go. You're gonna need it. But I tell you what, I'm taking Tommy's lace-ups with me and your high-water trousers too—a penance for good measure."

Bart opened the closet door and stepped out. "All right, I'll take my lumps. Be quick about it then." *No use drawing it out.*

5

THE MARKET OF PRICELESS TREASURES

Ten-year-old Sammy Nichols saw a strange flea market on the way back from middle school. It was in a previously vacant lot, surrounded by a high chain-link fence with a small opening. Above the opening was an archway made of dried branches and vines. Over the archway was a sign. It read "Market of Priceless Treasures and Bargains." He couldn't see through the links in the fence. His view was obscured by the many vines that had grown through the links. It was strange that the vines had grown there so quickly. They hadn't been there when he'd walked past the day before. Curiosity got the best of him. Sure, he was supposed to go straight back to the group home after school, but nobody would care if he was a little late. Tardiness was the least of their problems at the group home. Sammy walked through the opening in the chain-link fence.

The flea market was like none he'd seen before. Dozens of tables filled the space, holding many various items comprised mostly of secondhand housewares and clothing.

Behind each table stood a man or woman whom Sammy assumed to be homeless. All of the vendors wore some variant of a shabby robe. Some had a more modern look about them while others seemed well-worn. The shoppers seemed normal enough, browsing and haggling, many speaking in accents Sammy didn't recognize.

This place is weird.

Sammy approached the first table.

The dark-haired, olive-skinned proprietor welcomed him. "Ah, young man. How are you today?"

Sammy shrugged. "Hello. I'm okay. How are you?"

The man smiled and nodded. "Very good. Very good. I'm Amal. Welcome to my shop."

Sammy thought Amal was strange for referring to a broken-down table in a lot as a shop. "Thank you."

"I see you're confused. Is it your first time to the market?"

Sammy cocked his head to one side. "Yeah. I've walked past here before but have never seen it."

"We move quite often," Amal said. "Don't worry. You'll find us again."

Sammy was unsure if he wanted to find the place again. "Great."

"Do you like what you see?"

Sammy looked down at the table and saw about twenty dirty old bronze containers, most of which looked like strange gravy boats. "I'm really not looking for containers."

Amal shot Sammy a stern sideways glance but then burst into laughter. "Okay, boy, let me show you something else." He reached under the table and produced a small carpet. Then he unrolled it, laying it out over the brass and bronze gravy boats. "You see, the finest Persian rug money can buy." Amal ran a grimy hand over the rug.

Sammy also ran his small hand over the fibers. It felt soft and warm on the cool winter day. A warm breeze blew across the back of his neck. "It's very nice."

Amal looked Sammy directly in the eye, holding his gaze. "Yes, it is. What's your name?"

"Sammy Nichols, and my dad is a professional wrestler. He's tough. He beat Ivan the Bone Crusher last week at the Forum. Just saying." *In case you're a kid-grabber.*

Amal broke his gaze and laughed. "Well, congratulations to you both. Now, Sammy Nichols, are you interested in my Persian rug? I'll give you a good price."

"I like your rug, but I wouldn't have anywhere to put it. I'm only ten years old, and my family... we move around a lot." *No place for a rug in the group home.*

"Okay, Sammy Nichols. You don't buy now, but the next time you come to Amal's, come with heavy pockets. You'll be glad to see me then."

Sammy smiled, noting Amal's kind face. Amal returned the gesture.

Sammy waved and walked away from Amal's table, happy that he'd met him. Amal seemed nice. "Okay, Amal, see you next time."

Sammy wandered over to another table with a thin, long-haired woman standing behind it. He was more interested in the woman than the wares. He didn't even see what she was selling. He just wanted to talk to her. She looked nice.

"Hello, I'm Sammy."

She smiled and waved her hand over the objects on the table. "Hello, Sammy, I am Kassandra. Do you like what you see?" Her wide smile reminded him of one of the game show women who introduced the prizes on television. Sammy stared at Kassandra for a moment, then realized he was being rude and looked down to see the wares she was offering.

Dozens of cups, goblets, and all manner of plates and pottery filled the table. Sammy hadn't been the least bit interested in plates or cups but now thought he might like to know about them. "Where are these from?"

"Sammy, these are very old and very special. They're from Trigas. You can see the markings. They're genuine and the very rarest you'll find."

Sammy selected an earthenware cup. There were carvings on it, men with big thighs and fish. "How much is this one?" He didn't have any cash but held up the smallest, plainest earthenware cup anyway.

"We don't trade for money, Sammy. We trade for goods. Is it your first time in the market?"

He was deflated and placed the cup back down onto the rickety plywood table. "I don't have any money anyway." The salty smell of ocean and fish wafted up to his nose.

Kassandra smiled and looked away. "Then come back when you have something to trade."

Sammy felt invisible and thought it best to leave. It seemed that Kassandra wasn't interested in a friendly chat.

He moved on to another table, which held many interesting items. Sammy approached the table and was greeted by a short man with dark, oily hair and a long handlebar mustache.

The man smiled. "Hello and welcome. I am Pierre. Can I interest you in one of my timepieces?"

"Hi, Pierre. I don't have anything to trade. I'm just looking."

Many intricate-looking pocket watches and table clocks

sat on the table. Some of the clocks had their back covers open, and Sammy could see their intricate gears and levers. Amazed at the all the tiny moving parts, Sammy wanted to inspect one more closely but was afraid of breaking something.

Pierre carefully selected one of the pocket watches and held it for Sammy to see. "There's no harm in looking. Let me show you what I have. As you can see, the movement is perfect, the most accurate pocket watch you'll ever find. I should know, I have looked. You could go to the end of time and never find a more precise piece. Why, you could go to the end of time, and this piece will not have lost a beat. Clock makers these days with their atomics and their quartz computers, they have no love of the Craft, no respect. Time must be respected; it must be revered." Pierre paused.

"Um, I guess," Sammy said.

Pierre raised his eyebrows in mock surprise. "What would happen if you'd planned to travel on the midnight train to Paris, but you've gotten the timing wrong? You would miss the train, that's what would happen. We don't want to miss our trains, do we?"

Oh boy, here comes the lecture.

"But the subway comes every fifteen minutes, every five minutes during rush hour," Sammy said. "People don't use watches anymore. Every cell phone has a clock on it."

"Yes, but the subway doesn't go to Paris, does it? And what would happen if your subway was in the forest? Could you use your cell phone where there's no charging station? And if your trains were only scheduled to arrive just once during your lifetime? You wouldn't want to miss that train because of a depleted battery, would you?"

"No," Sammy said in a drawn-out tone, like he would

have done in school if the teacher had asked an equally silly question about equidistant trains and their arrival times.

"There are some moments that we absolutely cannot miss out on. What if I told you that your one true love would be here or there at precisely three o'clock in the afternoon and no later? Would you not make your best effort to meet your love?"

Sammy stared, hoping the lecture would be over soon.

"Men have gone to war; men have died for a chance to gain their heart's desire."

Sammy was unsure of what to say. He hadn't been in love, and another train always came along in fifteen minutes.

"Think about it, Sammy, and remember my name—Pierre, the master of time. I have to go now. I've a train to catch. I wish you well, and may you always have time on your side."

"Goodbye, Pierre."

Pierre packed his clocks away in wooden boxes filled with straw. Sammy left Pierre and his amazingly precise clocks.

A tall, thin man with long, dark hair and a short black beard caught Sammy's attention. The man eyed Sammy suspiciously from a few tables down the row. Sammy had seen that look before and thought it best to speak to the man before anything happened. Sammy approached the table.

The man's wide mouth grew into a wide smile. "Hello, young traveler. Welcome."

"I'm not going to steal anything," Sammy said. *Adults are always so suspicious with their accusing stares.*

"Why, of course you aren't," the man said coolly. "That'd be ridiculous."

Sammy placed his book bag on the table. That was what they did at the store. They held his bag so he couldn't smuggle any merchandise in it.

"Pardon my impropriety," the man said. "I was lost in thought. I didn't mean to be rude. I hope you can find it in your heart to forgive my transgression."

"Sometimes, before, when I went to a store with the other kids from the foster home, they would steal, and the store owner would think I stole too because I was with them, but I don't steal. You don't need to watch me."

The man bowed low with a knowing grin and a sparkle in his eye. "Again, apologies, young sir. Your face, it reminded me of someone from a far-off time. I meant no offense."

Sammy smiled back. "What are you selling?"

"Why, I trade in all manner of mystical and magical paraphernalia. Should you find yourself in need of a shrinking potion to make you as small as a mouse, I have one here. Should you find yourself lacking the proper ingredients for the perfect humble pie, I also have them here, minus the berries of course. They don't keep well."

Vials were arranged in neat rows on the table, and hard bound books were piled in high stacks. On the left was a wooden tray of dark, moist soil. It reminded Sammy of the trays that held baby tomato plants in springtime, except many different mushrooms sprouted from the soil. On the right, a pretty blue bird was perched in a tall, round bird cage, chirping a cheerful melody.

"Shrinking potion? You have a potion to make me as small as a mouse, like Alice's cake? You've got to be kidding. The other tables are full of old junk, and you're selling magic potions?"

The man chuckled. "Young sir, you'll find no junk at this market."

Sammy gazed over the multitude of trinkets, bottles, and vials on the wooden table. The strangeness of it all intrigued him. He enjoyed nothing more than a new oddity. This was better than the normal flea market, where he only found chipped commemorative plates and old cassette players. "What else do you have?"

The man held up a brown leather necklace with what looked like an old shark tooth pendant. "Take a look at this particularly precious piece. This is a Charm of Never Seeing. One could wear this pendant and walk through the world unnoticed, virtually invisible to those around you."

Sammy's heart jumped. It was the single greatest thing he'd ever heard. "This thing makes you invisible?"

"No, not quite invisible, just unnoticed by most. You'd still be recorded by modern surveillance equipment, and you'd alert any alarm devices."

"So people just won't notice you when you wear it?" Sammy asked.

"Most people, not all. I'd avoid hospitals, night clubs, the Balkans, and of course New Kent City."

Sammy's heart fell. Of course it was too good to be true. "Since we're in New Kent, it's kind of useless, but if most people can't see you when you wear it, what makes those places different?"

"I can see you are new to the arcane crafts. Let me explain something. The universe has a finite amount of magic and materials. When we want to collect some of that magic for ourselves, we need to take it from somewhere else or more precisely, in this case, from someone else. The particular magic in this piece came from the sort of person who wouldn't have given it willingly."

Sammy shot the man a chilling stare. "You mean this thing is stolen? I told you I wasn't into that."

The man pointed to the tooth on the necklace's pendant. "No, no. It's far worse than that. Let's just say these types of baby teeth won't fall out on their own accord." He buried the necklace deep in the folds of his dark-red robe then stepped back, folded his arms across his chest, and took a long, surveying look at Sammy. "Let me show you something more suited for your particular needs."

Sammy examined the trinkets and cases on the table, taking particular notice of a peculiar glass ball that looked a lot like a snow globe. "Sure, I like this weird stuff." He would be late getting back to the group home and would have extra punishment chores, but Sammy didn't care. This was too awesome.

The man took the glass ball from Sammy's hand. "Ah, I see you've found the Compass of Hearts." The glass ball changed immediately. While Sammy held it, the glass was obscure, but now the glass became clear. Inside the globe was an image of a beautiful dark-skinned woman whose brown eyes twinkled with hints of gold. The image changed, showing an old stone building, then it changed again. The globe now contained dark smoke, which gathered to a point near the glass just below its middle, where it was widest.

The man turned the globe every which way. He shook it, causing the smoke to dissipate and gather again. "You see, the smoke inside the globe gathers in the direction of your heart's desire." The dark smoke always gathered in the same area, pointing the way.

Sammy felt like he'd lost a game of magical Three Card Monty. Anyone who'd seen the guys down on Avenue B knew that it was impossible to find the queen. "That's cool. But why did it work for you and not for me?"

"It's not for you just yet. You may be just a bit too young for the compass. Something else, then."

Sammy looked over the table again hoping another of the curious objects would catch his eye. He picked up a black metal ring and placed it on his small finger. It was cold against his skin. Though he hadn't eaten anything since lunch four hours earlier, he tasted the metallic flavor of pennies.

The man's eyes went wide. "Ah, the Ring of Ogreish Might. Please be very careful, my wares are delicate, and you are not used to the strength the ring gives." The man, still smiling, slowly and carefully took Sammy's hand then easily slid the loose ring from his finger and exhaled.

"That ring gave me ogreish might?" Sammy asked. "I didn't feel very strong."

The man hid the ring inside his dark-red robes once again. "Feeling and knowing and being are all different things. I have some other items that might interest you. I'm willing to make a fair trade."

The man opened a small wooden box and removed three small pendants. He handed them to Sammy.

Sammy examined the tarnished metal pendants. "What are these?"

"These were given to me by an old wanderer a long time ago. He said they were very powerful charms of protection, and I'd find them a good home. I haven't been able to trace the source of their power, and as such, they may just be ordinary trinkets. I'll leave you to decide. I feel that trickster may have gotten the better end of the deal. As it is, I'd be glad to clear them from my inventory. Limited space, you know."

"What are the symbols?" Sammy asked.

"This one is the symbol Berkana, this one Wynn, and the

third, Algiz. That's the extent of my knowledge on the subject, I'm afraid. "

Sammy examined the small metal charms. The first, the Berkana charm, was small, square, and bronze in color. It felt heavy in the hand. The symbol looked like an uppercase B. The second, Wynn, was a dirty dark pewter of the same shape and size. The Wynn symbol looked like the letter P. The third charm was also small and squarish like the others but was a dingy yellowish color. The symbol Algiz resembled a lowercase T.

"I like them," Sammy said. "I'd like them, but I really don't have anything to trade."

The man smiled a sinister grin. "Everyone has something to trade—your firstborn child, your eternal soul. You see my point?"

Sammy stared at the man blankly. Unsure if the man had crossed a line, Sammy gave him a chance to explain before he bolted. The first rule of being a kid was to stay away from creepy old guys, but somehow the rules seemed different here in the market.

"Don't worry, I'm not going to cheat you out of your soul. These trinkets don't have much value, so I'll trade you for something equally worthless. How about three locks of hair? Does that sound fair?"

Sammy ran a hand up the back of his neck over the top of his head. "You want my hair?" He smoothed his unkempt mop to one side, confused that someone would want something that annoyed him so much. It never stayed where it was supposed to. "I'm growing it out for kids with cancer."

"It's more a token of good faith. I give you something I don't need, and you give me something you don't need. This is how business is done. We may see each other again when you do have something of value to trade. At that time, we'll both know that we can trust each other because we've done business in the past. It's how relationships work. You trust me, and I trust you. When that changes, we won't do business anymore, simple."

Feeling a bit like he was being set up for a long con, Sammy went along anyway. It was only hair, after all. "Sounds good."

A handful of market patrons had stopped by the table to browse. They cleared their throats simultaneously. The vendor also cleared his throat and handed the three charms to Sammy, who placed them in his pocket. The vendor produced a gleaming curved blade from inside of his robe. It was as long as Sammy's forearm. Sammy took the blade.

"Be careful," the man said. "It's a sharp blade."

"I'll be careful." Sammy used the knife, taking three tufts of hair from the top of his head, making sure to only cut away small bunches. He handed them to the vendor after he had cut them away. The cancer kids needed normal hair, not a chopped-up mess.

The vendor carefully placed each of the three locks in separate vials and stopped them up with a cork. When all the hairs were neatly tucked away inside his robe, the man cleared the table. "It was good doing business with you, Sammy. I look forward to trading again."

I didn't tell him my name.

Sammy looked around the market. All the other venders and patrons were looking his way. Some stole quick glances, while others stared outright. Sammy felt uncomfortable. He hated being watched. It made him feel guilty, though he knew he'd done nothing wrong.

"Until next time, young Sam. Goodbye," said the vender with Sammy's hair tucked quietly in his robe.

"Bye. Wait, what's your name?" Sammy asked.

"Oh, how rude. I'm Aja, the Deal Maker. Goodbye once more." Aja managed to pack up his table and trinkets and scurry through the makeshift door in the chain-link fence before Sammy could get in another word.

The staring subsided. Some of the onlookers shook their heads, but everyone went back to their own business. Sammy made his way out of the market, his three new trinkets safely in his pocket.

6

THE WAY IN

The run to the nature preserve should have taken Sammy ten minutes, but it took twenty. He got turned around and had to double back a few times, but finally, he was safely hidden behind the old oaks. That bloated cop wasn't going to find him in there. Sammy didn't feel as if he could stay hidden much longer. He had to get back and find Elizabeth.

That cop had said something about being on a time limit, so he had to hurry. The goon had said Sammy was beaten and they wouldn't let some kid stand in their way. The cop took Elizabeth. It was him. Sammy's life had never been threatened by the police. Was the guy even a real cop? He doubted it. City cop uniforms were blue, not faded purple as if they'd been sitting out in the sun for years.

He's an imposter. Probably got that uniform in a thrift store.

Sammy had to get back to that tunnel, back to the cell door. There had to be a way in. He would find it even if it took forever.

He stayed hidden behind the trees as he moved until he reached the edge of the nature preserve. The territory was all open fields after that. He would have to be quick and hope the fake cop wasn't looking for him.

Sammy ran most of the way back to the tunnel. He saw no sign of Captain Creepy or his cell phone. Sammy stood at the entrance to the tunnel before walking in. There were so many doors. If he couldn't get in through the cell door, maybe he could get in through one of the others.

He would check the cell door first. Maybe there was some clue as to what the heck was going on.

Sammy stood in front of the cell door with the broken white plate at his feet. He'd seen enough TV detective shows to know that he would have to use all his senses to find every clue he possibly could. The cell door was made of old rusty metal bars and had an ancient-looking lock. He tried forcing the bars apart, but it was no use.

He felt as if there might be a hall beyond the door, but it was so dark that he could barely see two feet past the bars. It was as though the darkness crept out rather than light penetrating in. He'd never seen anything like it before.

Trust your instincts.

Sammy listened, hoping to hear some sound that would give a clue as to how he might get inside. He heard the slightest sound of a howling wind. There had to be a hall beyond the door, and it had to be long, maybe another tunnel. But it wasn't windy that day. The opening on the other end had to be in a high place, really far away.

Sammy inhaled deeply, hoping to catch a whiff of some kind of clue. Sammy smelled beef. It was the most delicious beef he'd ever smelled. His mouth watered, and his nose pulled him closer to the bars. The aroma was irresistible.

His forehead hit the iron bar with a thud, causing him to snap back to reality. He looked for the steak, but it was gone. That must have been why Elizabeth was so crazy to get at that steak. It was no normal steak. Normal steaks didn't smell that impossibly good.

When Sammy had first gotten Elizabeth, the puppy had been so scared, she refused to eat the first whole day. Bob even tried feeding her a piece of steak, but she wasn't interested. That was when Jane read on the Internet that Yorkies didn't have a very good sense of smell compared with other dogs. Elizabeth had eaten the following day when she'd relaxed. There must have been something extra special about that steak in the tunnel that had made her go so mad.

Sammy was running out of senses. He needed to feel something. He ran his hands up and down the bars. They felt like old pipes, cold and hard. He felt around the ancient lock, hoping for a sign, but found nothing. The cobblestone floor was just like downtown, like the streets the city hadn't bothered to pave. It was all cold. The bars were cold, the cobblestones were cold, but it wasn't a cold day. That was a clue. Sammy had no idea how cold bars and stones would be helpful, but it was a start.

He'd learned that it was windy, cold, and weirdly dark behind the cell door.

He would have to find another way in. He didn't have time to stand around all day when they had Elizabeth. He did a one-eighty and looked at the door on the opposite wall.

It was a huge, sturdy wooden door, like a medieval castle door from the movies. It reached all the way up to the ceiling and had a sturdy-looking crossbar with a pull ring. *Wait.* Crossbars were usually on the inside of a door, not the outside. That was it. He could get in through that door.

Sammy grabbed the ring and pulled. He winced. His wrist still ached where Captain Creepy had twisted it. The crossbar must have been rusted, because it was stuck and didn't budge. Sammy pulled and pulled and pulled. *Still nothing.* Frustrated, he pounded on the door with his fists, hoping for some miracle. He was exhausted. He'd been pulling with all his strength and had none left.

He leaned his head against the door, tears streaming down his face. "No. No. No. I have to get in."

He fell to his knees, defeated and in agony over what they would do to Elizabeth. His palms pressed flatly against the rough wood as he slid down the face of the door, causing a two-inch splinter to jab into his open palm. He didn't care. It hurt, but he couldn't feel anything except grief for losing Elizabeth.

His hands came to rest on the crossbar. The runes on his bracelet clinked against the metal crossbar, echoing through the tunnel. A moment later, he heard the screech of metal grinding against metal.

Something had happened, but what? He raised his head, stood, and kicked the door in frustration. The crossbar rattled. It wasn't stuck anymore. He grabbed the ring again and pulled. The huge bolt slid free of its latch.

He pulled the door away from its frame. Billows of dust spewed out from behind it. Sammy stood in front of the huge open door but couldn't see inside. A curtain of darkness hung there. He had to go through. He had to find Elizabeth. Reaching his bloody hand out, he slowly walked through the door, watching his hand and arm disappear before his eyes as he stepped through into the darkness.

7

WARNINGS

Sammy stepped through the veil of darkness into a dimly lit room. The walls were made of large old stones, and he was reminded again of an old castle. Water seeped through the spaces between the stones and pooled in various spots on the similarly stoned floor. Torches hung on either side. A stone table sat in the middle of the room, looming like a monolith. It had a dark brownish-red cloth draped over the sides like an altar, and a piece of paper lay on it. The wall behind the altar was shaped like the letter V, and two huge doorless arches stood over tunnels leading in different directions. A plaque hung over each.

The small hairs on the back of his neck stood on end. He turned, startled. No one was there. Behind him was only the darkened doorway he'd just walked through. The wall was bare except for a small inscription etched into the stone beside the doorway. It read "flee and never return." Sammy ran his fingers over the childlike letters. The grooves were deep. It was not a hastily written warning. The stone was the hardest and coldest Sammy had ever felt. Someone had put a lot of time into that etching. Touching the cold stone helped him realize how cold he was. His breath exhaled in a thick white steam, like in the dead of winter. His thin T-shirt provided little warmth.

He decided to examine the room further. If someone had taken the time to etch those words of warning into the stone wall, he needed to be careful. Fear rose up in his chest. His breathing came quick and shallow. His heart beat loudly in his chest, and his pulse reverberated in his ears. A burning heat flushed over his entire body. His ears burned. His fingers tingled, and then his legs quivered and gave out. He fell to one knee, barely able to see. His vision distorted into a blur, and he rested his forehead on one knee.

Through heavy, labored breaths, Sammy tried to pull himself together. "Fear is the mind killer. Fear is the mind killer. You can do this. Elizabeth needs you."

Lifting his head, Sammy saw a shimmering ghost staring down at him. The milky-white, shadowy figure towered over him, and his weighty head fell onto his knee once more.

Come on, Sammy. Get up. Breathe.

He breathed slowly, in through the nose and out through the mouth. His head cleared, and he was able to lift it off his knee. The ghost was gone. Sammy sat on his backside with his knees pulled up in front of him. His bottom was wet from the pooling of the weeping walls. He dabbed the cold water over his face and neck. After a minute of deep breathing, he stood, hoping his legs would cooperate. They did.

"You got this, Sammy. Let the fear pass through you." The mantra worked. His head was clear, and his vision was back to normal.

Great, now I'm cold and wet.

It wasn't a great time for hallucinations. He had to figure

out what the heck was going on and how to get Elizabeth back. He had to get going, but he didn't know which way. Two arches, two paths—which one would lead him to Elizabeth? He stepped to the arch on the left and felt the slightest breeze on his ear as he heard the faintest whisper.

"The Reins, the Morsels, the Shackles lie in wait. Time is short."

Sammy had no idea what the words meant but thought it best to proceed carefully. He walked to the arch on the right and stood in front of it. Again, Sammy felt the breeze in his ear and heard the whisper.

"Eternal imprisonment before you. Flee and be free."

Sammy had no idea what to do. He read the plaques over the arches, and they echoed the words that had just been breathed into his ear. They were clearly warnings, suggestions that he should turn around and leave, but he wouldn't. He was going to save Elizabeth. Two paths and two ghostly warnings.

Was the ghost warning me?

He thought the ghost had been a figment of his imagination, a symptom or hallucination caused by hyperventilation, but he wasn't so sure. It might have been a real ghost. The situation just got real.

Sammy was torn. He wanted to run and find Elizabeth as fast as he could but wasn't sure which way to go. Both paths seemed like the wrong choice.

He placed his hands on the stone altar, touching the red cloth, hoping for some sign of what to do. He felt the cool breath in his ear and once again heard the eerie whisper. "Go, live, die. Remain, captive, a wraith in the infinite of the Timeless Prison. The hours are marked. The pendulum is loosed. Upon its quieting, so will be yours."

"Ahhhh." Sammy had to get out of there, or he would be

trapped. The warning was clear enough. He had to save Elizabeth before time ran out. She'd been there longer than he had. He needed to hurry.

The only other thing on the altar was a piece of old papyrus, like those from the desert exhibit in the history museum. Sammy picked it up and read.

"Bring me the one who sees the way. It is the key to our escape, to our return, to revenge. Follow the signs. Be patient, be vigilant. Your reward will be great."

The note was signed with an F written in a fancy lower-case script. It looked like the rune on the park cop's wrist. He was working for somebody. He was trying to free someone imprisoned there, and Elizabeth was the key. Sammy had to save her soon. Who knew how they would use her?

Looking once again at the red cloth on the stone table, Sammy saw a small white patch on the cloth. Examining the cloth further, he came to a horrifying realization. The cloth was white. The reddish-brown color was dried blood. The person who'd signed with an F had no good intentions for Elizabeth.

8

A GHOSTLY VEIL

Bart squinted. "What are you about then, coming through them doors into my altar room? Treasure hunter? Time jumper? Mad old wizard got himself hold of a young boy? Everlasting life and all that? You ain't one them cultists, I can tell straight away, but I had enough of you nosey pokers coming into my home."

The boy intruder sprang to life and in one motion, turned and hurled a tightly clenched fist straight through Bart's chest. The swing passed through Bart as if he wasn't even there, the momentum causing the assailant to tumble onto the cold, wet stone floor.

Bart roared with laughter. "Calm down, kid. You nearly jumped out of your knickers. No need to get all worked up. I ain't gonna hurt ya."

The intruder picked himself up off the floor and stared at Bart, his jaw hanging low. "Who are you, and where's Elizabeth? I want to see her now."

Bart's smirk faded. "Look here, Mighty Fists, you ain't in no position to be making no demands, right? Taking into clear consideration that little fainting spell of yours, right, the one you've only recently recovered from, I think you should mind your Ps and Qs and respect your betters."

The intruder was steaming and about to pop. "I'm not afraid of ghosts, and I'm not afraid of you. In fact, you're the most ridiculous ghost I've ever seen. Where'd you get that silly accent and those stupid clothes? Tiny Tim rejects go on sale at the thrift shop?"

"Right. I'm a poor substitute for a proper Oliver Twist," Bart bit back. "I know that. I've come to terms with my lot in life. The question is, have you made peace with your maker? Because you just might meet him."

The intruder held his sharp tongue, and Bart thought it better not to escalate the already volatile situation any further before he knew who or what he was dealing with. No normal kid could find the tunnel or get through one of its doors. This kid was dangerous, probably a dark wizard.

"I'll tell you what, love," Bart said. "How about I pull down my veil, and you promise not to do any more violence in my general vicinity. What do you say?"

The intruder agreed. "Yeah. I promise to cool out as long as you don't try anything funny."

Bart muttered the incantation, releasing the veil and bringing him back to his normal corporeal self. "How's that, then? All better? Now let's start with the questions. For one, who are you, and who's your master? For two, what do you think you're doing here? And for three, you think you can beat me?"

The intruder stared with big eyes, feigning surprise, an obvious deception. It had been decades since any other living person had set foot in the altar room, let alone a kid who looked not much younger than Bart did.

"I'm just looking for my dog," the intruder said. "I don't

want any trouble, really. I just want to get Elizabeth and go home."

Bart crossed his arms. "You're telling me you ain't of the Craft? You and your family? You're saying you ain't knowing of that other bloke, that buffoon who thinks he gonna come here and confuse me, and make me derelict in my duties? Is that what you're telling me?"

"The fake cop stole my dog," the intruder said. "I just want her back."

Bart spat on the puddled stones. "Yeah, I know that filth. He's a real copper though, of sorts. Squirrel chaser, not a proper crime fighter. He'd been sniffing around here for going on twenty year or so, him and his kind. Every few years, one of their kind find their way in by method or by chance."

"You've been haunting this tunnel for twenty years?" the kid asked, straight-faced.

Bart held his arms up, displaying his solid form. "I ain't no ghost. Can't you tell a proper wizard when you got one standing square in front of you? Your master done you wrong. Didn't teach you a thing, did he? I suppose that's how it goes sometimes. I knew a little of that... a long time ago."

The intruder paced back and forth, hunched over, rubbing his arms. "I'm really just a kid from the group home. I don't know about masters or anything like that."

Bart shook his head, unsure of the kid and his dog. "All right, all right. I knew you wasn't no wizard when I first peeped you walking that little mutt of yours. Your little pup walked right through the lightning gate, not a care in the world. And you don't even see the blue bolts arching over your head." *We'll figure out your little trick.*

The intruder's brow furrowed in epiphany. "You mean the lampposts? She cried when we first passed them."

Bart counted on his fingers. "I said I was watching, didn't I? I know everything that goes on in this park—who's coming and going, who the players are, the séances at the gazebo, the bloodsuckers, and the dogs toughing it out over by the amphitheater. I'm privy to all that and much more. But this part is mine. These hills, these tunnels, all mine. Nobody come into my house and get away with it."

"Except the cop," the intruder said flatly.

Bart looked away and chuckled. "Yeah, right, except the copper. But he ain't working alone. He got help, don't he? I couldn't see him. I couldn't find him on my compass, bloody cultist, always trying to relive the past."

A quizzical expression flashed across the intruder's face. "He's a cultist?"

Bart waved a hand at the door and stone walls. "Don't you know? This here is a prison. These doors, the lamp posts, and much more, are all designed to keep one man in, Lord Durga. But these cultists, see, they show up every few years, got some new plan to free Durga. It's my job to make sure they don't. I'm the caretaker."

"The cult cop is going to use her, isn't he?" the intruder asked. "But how?"

Bart rubbed his chin stubble. "It looks like that might be the case. Your wee pup is the first to find the tunnel in decades. Cute little mutt. That's why Culty Copper got his grubby hands all over her. He needs her to free Durga."

The intruder's eyes pleaded. "You can find her, right? You're the caretaker. You know this place. You've got to help me. Time is running out."

He almost felt bad for the kid and the dog, if they were in fact only a normal kid and dog, which wasn't likely. "You got that right. Clock's ticking out, shorter than you know. Time runs funny here, some days shorter, some longer. Who knows how long it'll be before that scum works it all out. It could be tomorrow or next week. For all I know, he could be shaking hands with the devil as we speak. Your Elizabeth, her hours are numbered. You've got to come to terms with that."

The kid hurried to the arches, seemingly impatient for Bart to follow. "Come on, then. Let's go. Take me to her if you can find her. What are you waiting for?"

Bart's ears flushed, infuriated that the bumbling idiot was able to infiltrate his impenetrable prison and was well on his way to freeing the one and only Lord Durga. Bart had failed. His only purpose in life was to keep the prison safe, and he hadn't even gotten that right. If only his master had taught him better.

"Take it easy, Speedy Feet. See, the thing about that is, I lost my compass. We've gotta take it slow. Don't want to lose our way, do we? That tosspot copper got himself a right good plan, don't he? Your dog and my compass, gone missing all in the same day. We find him, we find my my compass and your dog. And when we do, I got something for that wanker." Bart breathed slowly to calm himself and collect his energy. A proper wizard was always in full control of his emotions and energy. He desperately wanted to be a proper wizard.

The room shook. An eerie voice whispered in their ears. "The Legion of Stone lies in wait."

9

THE CARETAKER

Sammy's eyes popped wide. "What the heck was that? Legion of Stone?"

The pallid caretaker brushed the auburn hair from his coffee-colored eyes. They matched his tattered brown suit. "I just told you. This here is a prison; those be the guards. As far as their marching orders, I don't know nothing about that."

Sammy's legs quivered once more. *Hold it together, Sam. He's not a ghost. You're going to get through this.* Sammy rubbed his wrist. Touching the runes always gave him comfort. He needed comfort right about then.

The ghost-kid narrowed his eyes. "Hold on there. I thought you said you wasn't of the Craft? What's those runes there then in your hand? Let's see."

Sammy sprang back to his normal quick manner. He jumped across the room, putting the altar between the two. "Stay away from me. These are mine, and you're not getting your hands on them."

Besides Elizabeth, the runes were the only thing in the world Sammy really cared about. He felt that in some way they'd been made just for him, even though that couldn't be true. He would even have chosen them over Bob and Jane.

The caretaker stood tall, sticking his chin out. "Look here, kid. If you don't stop mucking about, I'm gonna have to get serious. Let's talk like proper adults here, everything on the up and up, all right?"

Sammy nodded, desperate to start searching for Elizabeth. He thought about making a break for it through one of the two arches, but the caretaker was his best hope for finding her. He had no choice but to cooperate.

Ghost-kid raised his hands, showing his empty palms. "My name's Bartholomew Baker, Bart for short. What's yours?"

Sammy relaxed the tension in his legs. "Sammy Nichols."

Bart pointed. "All right, Sammy, let's talk. You're not in the Craft, I know that. But you're working with someone, ain't you?" His eye movements were quick, darting to Sammy's hands and back up again.

Sammy's heart pounded, the throbbing in his ears grew louder, and the tingling in his hands retuned. "No. I told you."

Bart lowered his pointer finger and examined it, picking dirt from under the nail. "Come on with it. I know how it goes. Group home, you said? I know a little about that. I told you my name was Baker, but I didn't say how I come by the name." His expression softened. "Me mum drop me off in a little basket, all Moses-like, right in the bread man's cart. Imagine the shock on his face, come back from the mill, and look at what you got here with your sack of flour, a right little tyke. Well, I stay with the Bakers for a while. They push me off on the Donnellys, then the Smiths, and so on. That's the story, at least."

Bart examined the etching in the wall. "I left the workhouse sometime around five years old. Figured I was better off on my own, and I was at first. Once in a while, some bloke would come around, talk me into believing he'd help me out, keep me in milk and honey. You know what I mean? Turned out, them blokes were always more trouble than they're worth." He raised his eyebrows. "That's what happened to you, ain't it? Some old codger promised you a peek at his spell book, or something better?"

"Ugh." Sammy threw his hands up. "I told you, I'm not working for anyone. I live with my foster parents. They got me Elizabeth when I went to live with them. I got the runes at a flea market. I don't know anything about all this."

Bart scowled. He walked to the altar, picked up the parchment, and tossed it to Sammy. "Look here, Sam. You see that there? That's a feoh, Durga's mark. That's a rune. Runes have power. You mistake me for an idiot. You come here through the lightning gate with your dog. Your dog has more aura than most wizards I've seen. And now, you're sporting not one, but two runes of power, and on your casting hand to boot."

Runes have power? Sammy thought there might be some truth to that. "I got them at the flea market." *The door. It was locked. Did the runes open the door?*

Bart guffawed. "You got runes of power at a market?"

Sammy placed his hands on his hips. He hated being called a liar. "There was an arch and a sign. It was there one day, then it disappeared. The sellers were hobos and sold junk. I'm not lying. It was the Market of Priceless Treasures and Bargains."

Bart shook his head. "You're having a laugh. Think it's funny, do you? You expect me to believe you've been to the Market of Priceless Treasures?"

Sammy crossed his arms. Elizabeth was gone, and Bart only cared about runes and markets. "I got them from a guy, Aja."

Bart snorted. "You're pulling my leg. You seen Aja? But he's just a legend. My master gone batty looking all over for that Deal Maker, with charts and maps and all kind of date books. He gone halfway around the world, ten time over for that market. Said Aja wasn't even a man, something different."

Sammy shrugged. "He seemed okay to me."

Bart's eyes grew wide. "And what could you possibly have to broker a trade with Aja, orphan boy like yourself?"

Sammy shifted his weight from his right leg to his left and back again. "I gave him some hair. He said the runes were worthless."

Bart leaned closer, his eyes the size of dinner plates. "He wanted your hair?"

Sammy straightened up and balled his hands into fists. Elizabeth needed him. He didn't have time to deal with another bully. "I paid for these runes, and you're not getting them. I've beaten bigger kids than you, and I can do it again. I'm not afraid of you or your magic."

Bart stepped back. "We made a deal, remember? No violence. I ain't gonna take your runes. I ain't no thief... anymore. Anyway, two heads are better than one. If we're gonna find that copper, we gotta work it all out together. And if the Aja wanted your hair, well, he don't come out and play for just anyone. You might be a wizard after all... or maybe worse."

Sammy exhaled, relieved he wouldn't have to defend himself against Bart, the boy wizard. "Can they help find Elizabeth? The runes?"

The cool breeze whispered in Sammy's ear once again.
"The minutes pass, but how long will they last?"
A loud chime rang out that sounded like a church bell.

10

EMPLOYMENT

The servant's bell jingled. Bart jumped into action, straightening his bow tie as he flew up the stairs to the study.

"Yes, sir, what can I get you, sir?"

The master was handsome, with dark eyes and a strong jaw. "Bartholomew, be certain to provide all the usual comforts to the Count and his people. They should want for nothing. Do you understand me?"

Bart had only recently come under the employ of his new master. "Yes, sir. I understand, sir. I'll arrange for all the comforts and pleasantries, all the amenities. I'll provide no less than the best for your friends, sir. A better footman you won't find. I'll care for them just as I would for yourself, sir. And I want to thank you for giving me a place in your home, under your roof, sir. I haven't eaten this well in all my life."

He waited for some kind of response, some sign that the master had heard him. None came. A minute later, he plucked up the courage to speak again. "Very well, sir, if that is all, I'll return to my duties."

A piercing pain shot through Bart's head. He clenched

his eyes shut. In his mind's eye, he saw his master's face then the white-hot lightning. The bolts came from somewhere inside him, attacked, and in a flash, were gone. He fell to his knees and spewed sick over the floor. His breath seized, and his lungs collapsed. The pain was unbearable. He tried to scream but couldn't. All he could manage was a whimper, and he fell to the floor, unconscious.

Bart awoke minutes later with the master looming over him, looking down with eyes full of fire and hate. "Get up. Clean yourself and clean this mess. When you've finished, see to the task I put you about. And Bartholomew, never ever even think of affording another the same level of respect that is due me alone. I alone am your master."

Bart looked at the man's shiny black leather shoes. "Yes, sir."

The master was a hard man, a cruel man, but he gave Bart a home, a place he would be safe. It was worth it. Suffering under the barbarism of one man was far less painful than enduring the endless tribulations of the whole world. How many scars littered his body? How many times had he barely survived the street, brushed impossibly close to death? With this man, hard as he was, Bart had only to learn his lessons once. Once Bart knew what the master wanted, he would be able to make him happy. Then the master would be kind.

11

STREAMS OF SHEPHERDS

"How long do minutes last?" Sammy asked. "What does that mean?"

"It's the prison," Bart said. "It's always blurting out cryptic messages like that. Means we gotta move quick, that's all."

"Fine, we'll work together, then. Let's go," Sammy said. "But you lost your compass?"

"It don't make no never-mind. All them doors exit to the same place. I have an idea of where he's going."

"You sure?"

"Of course I'm sure. I told you I was the caretaker, didn't I?"

He's lying. Sammy was unsure if the thought came from his own mind or came from outside himself. "I've got no choice but to trust you, do I?" Sammy asked. He approached the arch to the left, taking one last look at the plaque over the door. The word "shackle" made him nervous. With his hand out in front of him, he walked through the sheet of darkness.

He stepped through to the other side, right into the

middle of a quickly moving stream. Bart was right behind him, but the archway wasn't.

The water was cold. The rushing of the stream echoed. A beam of sunlight shone down from far up above. It lit the stream and only the stream. Everything else was darkness. A bright-red fire flared up in the distance then quickly faded. Someone screamed, echoing far in the distance.

A chill ran up Sammy's spine. The small hairs on his arms stood up. "What is this?"

"Stay in the water. We don't want any of that, do we?" Bart said.

The warm sun soothed Sammy's clammy skin. The beam shifted, lighting a stone path off to the left side, leaving him and Bart in darkness with the freezing water rushing up to their shins.

"Let's go this way," Sammy said. He really wanted to get out of the cold water, out of the darkness and back into the warming rays. He felt a hand on his shoulder and jumped.

"Listen carefully," Bart said. "Stay in the water and walk straight ahead. If your foot touches one bit of land, we're gonna have to turn around and double back, so go slow."

They heard another drawn-out scream. The ray of sunshine expanded, moving up the path, resting on an opening in the stone wall. Sammy looked through the opening and saw grass and fruit trees. It was an orange grove, but looked like one in an old painting or a pleasant dream.

"Never mind what you think you see. It's not where we're going. Easy does it, straight ahead." Bart squeezed Sammy's shoulder.

The oranges looked delicious, so juicy. Sammy imagined how good the warm grass would feel on his feet. He desperately wanted to lie in it. Just a little nap couldn't hurt. Elizabeth might be in there, in the grass.

Another bloodcurdling scream echoed through the darkness, jolting Sammy back to the task at hand.

"See there? He ain't knowing about the stream. Sure, it's wet and cold, but it's far better than what he's up to."

"Is that him, the park cop?" Sammy asked. "Did he go to the grove?"

"Yeah, it's him, the filth. I doubt he saw a grove, though. Who knows what sort of oasis that bugger conjured up. For me, it's a carnival, one like I saw as a kid. I only went into the oasis once, don't know how long I rode that merry-go-round. Could've been years. Only got out when some other bloke stumbled over me and woke me up. Didn't even see me sitting there. Poor chap, he didn't last too long after that."

Sammy jumped at the sound of rustling autumn leaves, then a snap, and another. Several huge German shepherds snapped at him from the right edge of the stream, their snouts and sharp fangs only millimeters away.

Bart's hand clamped down tighter on Sammy's shoulder. Sammy trembled. He wanted to run to the grove, to the warm grass, where it was safe. He took a deep breath, concentrating all his will on one thought. *Don't run.*

"You see? It's all a game," Bart said. "Nothing to be afraid of. They ain't gonna get you. I saw dock workers, what did you see?"

"Dogs."

"Let me guess, nothing like your little sweetheart?"

"No," Sammy said. "More like the kind who'd have her as a snack."

Only two weeks prior, while walking Elizabeth on the street, he'd had an unfortunate run-in with a particularly ravenous shepherd. It came out of nowhere, snarling and vicious. Sammy had no choice but to scoop little Elizabeth up in his trembling arms and hop onto the nearest auto, an Econoline van. The dog's owner eventually came along and got the beast under control. But what was done, was done. He'd had nightmares for a week.

The snarling shepherds jumped into the stream, blocking Sammy's path. He stopped. "They're in the water. What do I do?"

"My dock workers are here too. Just keep walking. They won't hurt ya."

Sammy took another small step. The dogs withdrew an inch, still snapping. He took another step. So did they.

The grove. She's in the grove.

The thought wasn't his own but came from outside his mind. He was sure of it now. It was accompanied by the faintest of voices, deep and hollow.

"What are they saying? The voices? You been hearing them, haven't you?" Bart asked. "You ain't believing 'em. I can tell."

"No."

The snarling dogs still snapped at Sammy. More of them now, dozens, growled and barked in the darkness.

"Mine been saying to knock you over your head. I ain't done so yet."

"Thanks," Sammy said. *Maybe he isn't so bad, after all.*

The dogs retreated. The sunlit orange grove faded. A dim light glowed under the water. The rushing stream slowed to a trickle. Then the water stopped flowing altogether.

There was a hole in the gravel. Sammy looked down into the hole and saw the shattered plate and the cell door. The hole in the stream bed was a passage through the tunnel's ceiling. "It's the tunnel with the doors. It doesn't make sense. There's a bridge over that tunnel. We can't be on top of it."

"You just figuring this out now? You're a regular Galileo Galilei, aren't you? Of course it don't make sense. It's magic, the arcane arts. I understand if you've got cold feet. That's your way out, there." Bart knelt down and plucked a mushroom from the gravel. He sniffed it and put it in his breast pocket.

"No, I'm not leaving," Sammy said. He stepped around the hole and continued on the dried stream bed.

The darkness receded. Sammy saw the cop on a stone platform at the end of the stream bed. He held Elizabeth in his filthy hands.

Sammy tried to run, but Bart held him back.

He had Elizabeth. Sammy had to save her. The cop was burned. His face was charred, and his clothes smoldered. He stood in front of a doorway. The doorway was carved in the cavern wall. It was shaped like a man's face. The face was screaming in agony.

"Hold it right there, kids," the cop said. "One more step, and the dog gets it."

Elizabeth writhed in the cop's arms. She yelped and howled, trying to escape. She barked and bit. He tucked her small body tighter under his arm, like a football, one hairy hand on her tiny neck.

Sammy gasped. There she was. He had to get to her. But how? He was unable to speak, unable to move.

Use your words like Dr. Z taught you. "No. You stop. If you hurt her—"

"Go back home, kid," the cop said. "Time's up. There's nothing you can do about it."

Sammy shoved Bart away, breaking the grip on his shoulders. He sprinted and bounded up on the stone platform. He grabbed the cop's arm, pulling at it, hoping to break Elizabeth free, but it was no use. The man batted Sammy away. He flew several feet and fell to the ground, hitting his head on the damp stone. His vision blurred. He got up onto his feet but fell back onto his backside, too dizzy to do anything but sit there, blinking and watching.

The cop held Elizabeth tightly and ran through the screaming door in the cave wall. The mouth closed behind them. They were gone.

12

NIGHTSHADE

The master sat at a table in the dimly lit room of curiosities. "Bring the essence of nightshade." Old books, scales, and devices lined the shelves. Bart could only wonder at their purpose.

Quickly and quietly, Bart shot to the cabinet of ingredients. "Yes, sir." He carefully selected one of the vials, hoping he'd guessed correctly, and sped back to the master without making a sound. The difference between walking and running is a subtle art. He would never forget what it had cost to learn that lesson.

Bart placed the vial on the worktable next to the other ingredients. There was also a black leather tethering leash on the table, but Master didn't own any dogs. He knew well enough that he shouldn't see anything he wasn't invited to see and averted his eyes. "Your nightshade, sir."

The master's eyes were fixed on the tabletop. "I said the nightshade. This is wolf's bane."

Bart sped back to the cabinet, collecting another vial at random. "B-B-Begging your pardon, sir. My mistake. I'll do better next time."

"No need. I'll do it," said the master. Bart watched the clear glass vial of crushed green herbs sail through the air with the silky smoothness of a bird in flight. It came to rest on the workbench without so much as a clink.

Bart studied that vial. The green-and-brown contents were forever burned into his mind.

"Did you see which one?" the master asked.

Bart closed his eyes, recalling the vial of herbs. "Yes, sir. Top shelf, second from the right, bottle two inches tall, dark cork. Contents, brown and green, finely crushed, purple flecks throughout."

The master nodded in approval. "Very good. This past year, you've come a long way. I'm pleased with your performance. I've no doubt that one day you'll grow into a great practitioner of the art."

The man raised his head and looked at Bart standing beside the bench. "You're wondering why I haven't taught you about the vials yet. You question the purpose of all these strange implements. Let me start today. Nightshade is a powerful sedative. It causes any man to fall into a deep slumber. When combined with other powerful ingredients, it can work wonders." The man uncorked the vial and poured some of the nightshade onto one side of an apothecary scale.

Bart committed the herb's purpose to memory. "Nightshade for sleep, sir."

The master leaned back in his chair, held his hands out in front of him, making a pyramid, his fingertips barely touching. "Let us take the man-catcher herb. Alone, it renders a patient very open to suggestion. When combined with nightshade and a few others, it puts the patient into a special kind of deep sleep. In that state, we can whisper sweet nothings in the patient's ear, and he'll experience wildly vivid dreams and hallucinations in accordance with the graphically detailed sweet nothings we previously spoke of. He'll have no memory of this dream, only a wild fire in his heart to recapture it. What does this tell you?"

Bart bowed, avoiding eye contact. "Thank you, sir, and begging your pardon, sir, I do not wish to seem impertinent, but I believe it tells me why so many of our frequent dinner guests often stay in their rooms until well after ten the following morning."

The master laughed. "You're quite right, and I'm willing to wager you thought it was an effect of Mrs. Beesley's roast."

Bart exhaled and chuckled. "I did, sir."

13

——————

AURAS

The dry riverbed under Bart's feet faded away. He closed his eyes and concentrated on the discernment of true intention spell. He saw only the aura, the life force of every living thing in his purview. The aura surged and pulsed, the energy and power flowing over the earth and the stone platform.

SAMMY'S AURA glowed a pale yellow. He was an innocent.

The cop was gone, but his deep-burgundy aura trail remained, streaming through the Madness Gate.

"WHAT ARE YOU DOING?" Sammy screamed. "Wake up! They're getting away!"

BART WASN'T interested in chasing down the insane police officer just yet. He was interested in seeing the true nature of things. He was interested in Elizabeth Bennet. She was the key to all of this. What was it about her that made her able to enter the prison, and what did they want with her? After all, she was just a dog.

HER AURA OVERSHADOWED THE OTHERS. It was bright and large, consuming the other colors. Sammy's yellow and the cop's red blended into her blue then were absorbed by it. The trace she left behind was less of a trail and more of a cloud, momentarily engulfing the cavern before it dissipated.

SAMMY SHOOK Bart by the shoulders, jostling him out of his trance. "What are you doing? We need to get her. Come on, through the mouth!"

BART SHOVED SAMMY AWAY, coming back to full awareness. "Get your grubby hands off me. We'll get her. Don't worry. I got it all figured it out."

SAMMY POINTED an accusatory finger at Bart. "You got what? You have nothing figured out. That dumpy creep is getting away, and you're standing here taking a nap."

BART INHALED DEEPLY AND BLINKED, his eyesight adjusting back to normal. "I wasn't sleeping. I was seeing through the third eye. Besides, the Madness Gate's on a timer. We can't get through just yet. It'll take a minute. We've got to wait it out, until it opens back up. Nothing to do about it."

. . .

"WHAT THE HECK are you talking about? That's, that's..."

BART NODDED. "Insane, I know. It's called the Madness Gate, after all." His voice softened. "Sammy, I've got to come clean about something. I've been a hair less than totally honest. I lied about my compass. Culty don't have it. I've got it here in my pocket."

CONFUSION clouded over Sammy's face.

"I DIDN'T TRUST you before, but I do now," Bart said. "I executed a spell of seeing. It showed me what I needed to know. Your aura, it's clean, mostly."

SAMMY'S EYES POPPED WIDE, and he threw his hands up. "So you've been lying to me the whole time? You've been accusing me of lying, but it was you being dishonest all along? What else have you been lying about?"

"I DIDN'T CHANGE NOTHING. We still had to catch up to Culty either way. He's looking for Durga. Won't be hard to catch up with him. I didn't need the compass for that. Besides, I couldn't do it earlier. I needed you and Culty together to see how your auras played off each other's, to see if you were working with him. Auras of a feather flock together. You know what I'm saying?"

. . .

SAMMY SHOOK HIS HEAD. "I told you I wasn't with him."

BART NODDED. "I know, but trust don't come easy to a person in my position. And I think I riddled out why Durga wants your Elizabeth."

SAMMY'S CHEST WAS HEAVING. "Is he going to hurt her?"

BART PUT a soft hand on Sammy's shoulder. "He won't do nothing without Durga, that's for sure. But what I think is happening... I think they need to use her as a cloak."

SAMMY LISTENED WITH BATED BREATH.

"YOU SEE, her aura was so bright and grew so large, it consumed the others, yours and his," Bart said.

SAMMY'S FACE crinkled in confusion.

"I THINK Culty is planning on using her as a shield against the prison walls. This here prison employs magical fields of detection. That's why Durga can't leave. It senses his aura and employs a multitude of barriers and redirections to keep him inside. He knows all about 'em and how they work. Now if your Elizabeth, if her aura is so powerful, it consumes the auras of those around her, it might make Durga undetectable, leaving him able to walk right out. I reckon Culty caught sight of your Elizabeth and snatched her up with that in mind."

SAMMY EXHALED A SIGH OF RELIEF. "That's good. He won't hurt her, then."

"IT AIN'T GOOD, and you need to prepare yourself for the worst."

AN EXPRESSION of panic and disbelief crossed Sammy's face. "But you just said he needs her."

BART LOOKED AWAY. "For now, he does, but who knows what that batty bastard'll do in the future."

SAMMY SHOOK HIS HEAD. "What do you mean?"

BART'S TONE was low and solemn. "It's what he does, what they all do. When they want to learn about something, to recreate it..."

SAMMY'S VOICE was barely audible. "I get it. Like the frogs in school and cosmetic testing on cute little bunny rabbits."

. . .

"I'm sorry, Sammy." Bart's voice brightened in an attempt to sound like one of those confident, inspiring generals he'd eavesdropped on in his youth. "We won't let it come to that. We're gonna find your Elizabeth and get her safe, and I'm gonna make certain that copper and his kind know who they're dealing with. When I'm done, they'll know to never come back again."

Sammy's voice sounded like a small child. "But you can find her, right?"

Bart took the small pocket-watch-like device from inside his shabby brown jacket and handed it to Sammy.

Sammy inspected it. "It's an old watch."

"It only looks like a watch," Bart said. "Open it up and see what it shows you."

The cool breeze whispered in their ears once more. "The hours grow short."

14

LESSONS

The master took Bart by the shoulders, smiling widely. "First things first. Welcome home. I've a splendid dinner planned to celebrate our second anniversary. It's been two years since I found you in that terrible state. You've come a long way, my boy. Made me proud. I've many great plans for your future, but that's for later. Tonight is about remembering the good things, the accomplishments you've achieved. Sit." The master sat behind his desk in the study. "Bartholomew, tell me, how was your journey? What news did you gather?"

BART SWELLED with pride and sat opposite his master. "Sir, I was able to gather information, lotta good stuff, troop movements, crop yields, everything you asked for. I've got it all right here in my head. No more note-taking, sir. Again, thank you for correction in that matter. I sat in on the meeting just like you instructed. I heard it all, all the plans, every juicy little morsel these Yanks are getting up to."

. . .

THE MASTER NODDED HIS APPROVAL. "Excellent. You did very good. I'll have something special for you in your room tonight. You deserve it."

BART LOOKED DOWN, his voice quieting slightly. "Just one thing, sir. If I could be so bold..."

THE MASTER'S eyes narrowed into slits as he studied Bart intently. "What is it?"

"SIR, my veil. It was a long meeting. It held out for the duration, and I got all you asked for. But after the meeting, a couple blokes hung around, talking about their wives and such. They were old friends. I could tell by the way they clasped hands. I tarried about, hoping to catch a scrap. You never know what could be said between a couple old pals. Well, it seemed they were getting on about something good. Their voices got all hushed and such. I was all set to get in on the big news, you know, always wanting something extra for my master."

BART FIDDLED with the buttons on his jacket. "Then me veil gave out, just for a moment, mind you. They didn't see me, but the disturbance was enough to move them along. The older gentleman said something about getting a chill, and they went on. I lost my morsel."

. . .

THE MASTER EXHALED. "You care for more lessons, I'm well aware. We've spoken of this. You must be patient. I'll instruct you so far as your need. As it stands, your veil will do for now. We can discuss furthering your education when the time comes."

15

INTO THE MOUTH OF MADNESS

Sammy opened the pocket watch. "It's pointing at the mouth."

Countless tiny gears spun and whirled at amazing speed. A compass rose was etched in the glass, covering the gears. A single large hand pointed the way.

Bart nodded. "Right, that's where we got to go. It points to evil, the most evil in its area of detection."

Sammy imagined what it would point to on the streets of New Kent. "What's its range?"

Bart shrugged. "I don't rightly know, but I know ever since I had it, it's always pointed toward Durga, the most evil man I ever heard of."

Sammy marveled at the loud groaning sound of crushing stone echoing through the cavern. The Mouth opened.

Bart shot Sammy a steely look of determination. "Here we are. You ready? Stay behind me. Keep close and don't run off."

Bart walked through the Mouth Gate, and Sammy

followed closely behind. Once they were through, the mouth closed, leaving only a flat cave wall where it had been.

They stood in a cave.

"Come on," Bart said. "Let's be quick about it. I been through here before with my duties as caretaker, and it's no place for games."

Arched passageways were carved in the cavern walls. Bright white light shone through the arches then faded. The archways led to other places. Some of them led outdoors.

Bart pointed straight ahead, down the cavern. "Don't even look. We don't need what's in them doors."

But Sammy looked. "It's you, and a man, and a woman. You're all wearing jackets and tall boots, riding horses."

Bart nodded but kept his eyes straight ahead. "Me mum and dad. Lovely people, I suppose. Never met 'em."

"Is it really them?" Sammy asked.

Bart shook his head. "No, they ain't, or they ain't real yet. I'm not sure. There's yours, lovely woman, your mum. You've got her eyes."

Sammy stopped in the doorway and stared at the tall, sophisticated woman. She wore a modest, elegant white dress and gold bracelets. Her teeth sparkled behind her kind, wide smile.

"See, you want to go there, don't you?" Bart asked. "Want to be with your parents who you've never known. Go on, live that perfect life. Forget about Elizabeth. She don't need you."

Sammy stood in the archway, transfixed on the woman and her kind face. He held up a hand, reaching for her. His hand passed through the arch's threshold. She caught his gaze and waved him over. He took a small step. She motioned to a table. A Thanksgiving feast was laid out with turkey and all the dressing he could imagine. She pulled a chair out for him. He took another small step.

"Sammy," Bart barked.

His mother turned to a man on her right, his father. He was tall with neatly combed hair, dressed in a pale-gray suit. The man pointed to a Christmas tree. He picked up a gift wrapped in bright-red paper and a gold bow. He held it out for Sammy. Sammy took another step.

"Sammy," Bart barked louder.

Several children sat under the tree, unwrapping gifts, showing Sammy what they had gotten. A boy, about his age, displayed the new video game system he'd received. The younger children unwrapped toy trucks.

"Wake up, kid," Bart yelled.

Elizabeth was there. She rolled around in the mess of wrapping paper, tossing it up in the air and catching it in her small mouth. She barked at Sammy as if to say, "Come, play with me." A huge spotted Great Dane lounged on the floor next to Elizabeth, its eyes calling to him.

Bart came close to him and spoke in unmistakably clear tones. "Sammy, listen to me. You think it's what you want, but it ain't. Your real life is here, not in there."

Sammy blinked and shook his head. He turned to Bart. "Wha... my life? What's going on here?"

Bart exhaled. "We're not totally sure. I've seen others go through and never come back. Don't know if they got what they wanted, what the door showed 'em. I never went through, though. It's not real. It's what we want, but it ain't what's right, them Doors of Desire."

They walked on. Sammy blinked and shook his head, clearing the confusion. Each archway showed them a different life they could lead if they quit their quest.

"I've spent a lot of time in here, considering this and

that," Bart said. "Cast many a detection spell in here, hoping to gain some insight."

"Into what?"

"The true nature of the doors and what's behind 'em."

"What did you come up with?" Sammy asked.

"Nothing. They're pure energy, pure magic, neither good nor evil. I can run through a litany of incantations, giving insight into the nature of things, what's good, what's evil. You see, people are good or bad. Most are both, somewhere in the middle. Some people try very hard to move one way or the other."

Sammy listened, hoping to gain some insight into the strange new world he'd stumbled into.

"You see, human beings are all about self-preservation," Bart said. "They do what they have to to survive. They're neutral. For me, I done wrong, but I never meant any harm. But some others, they go out of their way to be more good or more bad."

"Some people are just bad and don't have to go out of their way," Sammy said.

"Right. Lotta folks appear to be predisposed to the crueler side, but that's not the case. Villains are made, not born. As for Durga, I suspect he's a special case. But you see, the matter of it is, when we move away from neutral, we gain something, but it costs."

Off through one of the arches, Sammy's family was at the beach. The children had buried Dad and built a sand castle over him. He broke free, stomping around like a movie monster.

"Costs what?" Sammy asked.

Through another arch, Bart and his father had been chopping wood but stopped when his mother brought out a pitcher of fresh lemonade.

"Could be anything. Take it like this, say a bloke robs a bank and kills two people. He gets away. Now he's gained lots of money, but he lost much more. Now he's got two souls following him around, pulling him down into the muck."

Sammy squinted. "You mean the ghosts would haunt him?"

"It's a possibility, maybe, maybe not. But there will be a debt. The universe will pull him back to neutral for sure. Karmic debt, the Easterners call it. I'll give you an example. This one time, I nicked one of them penny-dreadfuls for a laugh. I couldn't eat it or wear it, mind you. I wanted it for no other reason but it wasn't mine. I couldn't even read. Later that day, I boarded a coach for the coast. That night, I discovered me good gloves had gone, must have left them on the box seat. Gone forever they were, and worth a lot more than that booklet."

"Guilty conscience," Sammy said. Through another arch, Sammy's family laughed over a picnic table in the park.

"How about the other way? Take your average spinster. You got some charlatan, talking about healing the sick and all that. Those phony healers been around since time began, medicine men and all. Well, some people... say an elderly widow with no heirs, say she got all wrapped up in the doings, and she want to make some good in the world. Now, she give all her money away, hoping to make life easier for some others, invalids or whatever. What's next is she's destitute on the street, beggin' for scraps. You see, it all comes back to the middle.

"I got wrapped up with a bloke like that once, had me begging for coin on the street, said he was soliciting funds to build a proper orphanage with schooling and all. Wasn't I taken aback when the constable dragged me in front of the magistrate, making all kind of accusations, accuse me of financing a criminal enterprise and what not. The swindler duped at least a dozen good men and women out of their purses. If the vicar's wife hadn't come to my aid and pled my innocence, it would have been the workhouse for me, for sure."

Sammy nodded. "Yeah, I get it."

Through another arch, Bart picked raspberries while his mother held a wicker basket. His father struggled to free the carriage wheel from a muddy rut. Bart scowled at the defiant carriage wheel. "Magic, energy, the universe. It's all neutral. People are good and bad, magic is pure energy, pure universe. It's not good or bad. Only the people who use magic can be good and bad. Some people are so good or so bad that the debt builds up. Them people are always trying to live forever. Probably Durga's plan."

"Why?" Sammy asked.

"They spend their whole lives running from it, the karmic debt. They know it'll catch up to them eventually, so they try to not die, to outrun it forever. Take Lord Durga, he's old. How old, I don't know. But when he finally passes, there'll be hell to pay. I've no idea what lies beyond, but when he passes to the other side, all the evil deeds he done, that karmic debt'll crash down upon him like a mountain."

They came upon another door of desire and heard a deep, droning voice from inside. It was a pathetic-looking man sitting on the stone floor. The rest of the room was obscured and blurry. The man wore filthy, striped prisoner's clothes. His dark hair and beard were long, splayed out on the floor beside him. He muttered in a low, droning tone. "The Lead, the Shackles, the Morsels, the Lead, the Shackles, the Morsels, the Lead, the Shackles, the Morsels."

Sammy stood behind Bart, peering over his shoulder. "Who is it?" he whispered.

Bart scowled and spit. "It's him, Durga."

Sammy nudged Bart ahead, toward the arch and Durga. "Go. Go in. It's a short cut. If we get to him before the cop, then—"

"It's him, but it ain't," Bart said. "It's like your mum back there. The doors are showing us what we want to see, that's all."

Even though it was just a mirage and not really Durga, Sammy moved closer to get a better view of the monster who he'd heard so much about. He wondered how Bart knew all of this, how he'd come to be there as caretaker. He half expected to see Bart in there too.

Bart guffawed, pointing. "Besides, this here bloke ain't even a man anymore. Look at him, broken beyond repair, muttering on about who knows what."

Sammy checked the compass just to make sure it wasn't really Durga. It pointed straight ahead and not through the arch.

Bart shook his head and continued down the tunnel. "This is a waste of time, and time's running out."

They continued past the arches, finally coming to the end of the cave-like tunnel.

A shimmering mist hung in the air at the end of the tunnel, blocking the view of what lay ahead.

"Another magical entrance?" Sammy asked.

"One way only, that's the purpose of these strange portals. It's a big maze, keeping trespassers out and him in. I only know because I been round so long."

Sammy cocked his head to the side. "How do you know all this? How'd you get to be caretaker anyway? You're just a kid like me."

The cool breeze whispered in their ears once more. "The time draws close. Flee and be saved. Despair lies ahead."

"Come on, through the mist," Bart said, disappearing through the mist. Sammy followed.

16

ORDER IN THE COMMONS

Bart paced back and forth in the study, hands shaking, his voice quivering. "They was ready. They knew something was coming. Had about a hundred burly blokes milling about outside. They weren't a problem."

Bart sat, raised his hands to eye level, and examined them as if for the first time. "Once inside, my veil held up. They had a user in the chambers, young bloke. His craft work was rubbish, didn't notice me in the least. I strolled right past him."

Bart stood and walked to the open window, watching the groundskeeper tended a row of hedges.

Could be worse ways to spend your day.

"I did like you said," Bart said. "The whole vial in his sherry, every last drop. First gulp, Prime Minister drop to the floor, quick-like, convulsing and thrashing about. Doctor come rushing over. 'Nothing to do,' he said. The whole party up in arms, locked down the commons, they did. I rush out, no one the wiser."

Bart sat again. A raven landed on the open windowsill. It

cawed and flew off. Streams of red light filtered through the stained glass. He swallowed. "He's going to be all right, he is. He'll recover. It was just the nightshade, wasn't it?"

The master put a hand on Bart's shoulder. "Bart, you must bear up to this. It's for the best. The people, they need order. They need guidance. We can't have them running amuck, making the rules up as they go. You've done well."

"I never done nothing like that before, nothing so... evil." Bart stood and spewed sick all over his fine black leather shoes. "Did I kill that man?"

The master squeezed Bart's shoulder. "Listen to me carefully. Great men are made, not born. Not like a hammer to steel, or chisel and stone, but like a baker to bread. A man kneaded in the proper fashion and left to rise, in due course, will bake into greatness. You'll be a great man one day. I'll see to that."

The master slammed his hand down on the desk. "As we speak, there are those who plot and scheme our downfall. They desire our wealth, our power. They aim to take what is rightfully ours, to crush us underfoot. They would have us under their thumb. They elevate the heathen and bring us down low. My boy, be content in the knowledge that you do what's good and right."

17

THROUGH THE FLAMES

Sammy stepped out of the mist. Doors—hundreds, thousands of doors—filled the long, wide cave tunnel. The doors weren't in walls like usual. They floated on their own, without frames, without hinges. The long, wide tunnel gently sloped downhill. The doors were spaced sporadically throughout the tunnel. They faced every which way, some facing each other, some at odd angles. A revolving door squeaked as it circled endlessly.

Sammy's mouth hung open. "What is this?"

"The Maze of Doors, that's what I call it," Bart said.

Sammy followed Bart past dozens of doors, stirring up clouds of dust with every step. Bitter cold emanated from some, turning Sammy's breath to white puffs as he passed. The odd layout prevented them from walking in a straight line. They walked in a zigzag fashion, like in a crowded shopping mall.

"Why is it called a maze?" Sammy asked. "It's just a tunnel with doors in it. There's nothing to figure out."

"Oh, really? Well, let me ask you a question. How long have we been walking, and how many have we passed?"

Sammy raised an eyebrow. "About a minute, two dozen or so."

"Turn around then, Inspector," Bart said.

When Sammy turned, he realized that though they'd been walking, they hadn't gone anywhere. They were still at the start of the tunnel.

Sammy threw his hands up. "Come on!"

"I knew you'd get a laugh out of that," Bart said.

"Stop messing around," Sammy said. "You're wasting time."

"The look on your face was priceless." Bart laughed. "I'd pay two bits to see that again."

Sammy snorted. "So how do we get down the tunnel?"

Bart slid open a nearby Honshu paper door. "Through the maze, of course." He stood in front of what looked like a tall rectangular window with many square panes, except it had white paper where the glass would have been. It floated in the air and moved aside when Bart pushed it, as if it were on rollers. He stepped past the door and disappeared.

Sammy's mouth fell open. He tried to speak, but nothing came out.

Bart emerged from behind a glass shower door only feet away. "Over here, Inspector. See? You go through one and come out another, the way down the tunnel."

Sammy slid the Eastern paper door open and stepped through, exiting through the shower door a few feet away. "This'll take forever." The glass of the shower door was cold and wet. "There's a pattern, right?"

Bart pointed to several doors with dents and scratches. A rusty metal hatchway had at least two dozen hash marks scribed into it. "Thought I was done for more than once. Proper note-taking is the key to things like this, you see? Lose track, get turned about, and you're done for. Got so hungry, almost ate my shoe leather once. Took me years to puzzle it out, learn the layout, the rotating pattern. Coincides with the Seven Sisters, by the way."

"I'm glad you made it," Sammy said. "You mean Pleiades star cluster? We learned about them in astronomy class."

Bart chuckled. "You're brighter than you look, and you're right. The pattern changes with the movements of the heavens. And you wasn't glad to see me before by the way you run your fist through my face just then."

Sammy tapped Bart on the arm. "You're not all bad either, and you're not as tough as you talk."

Bart tapped Sammy on the arm just slightly harder. "You might be right about that. We'll see when we come to the end of the maze, won't we?"

Sammy was close on Bart's heels, going through the various doors, rushing to get through and find Elizabeth. "You scared me pretty good when I thought you wanted my runes." Winding through the maze seemed like an endless endeavor, but Bart was actually growing on Sammy, which made it a little better.

Sammy fiddled with his bracelet. He stared off at an old-fashioned black wrought iron elevator gate, the kind in the old pre-war buildings. "My runes, I think they're special."

"If you got a feeling about them, then you're probably right," Bart said. "We should always be trusting our feelings. When we get an inkling about something, it's the universe giving us a hint as to which way we should go."

He didn't before, but Sammy started to trust Bart. He trusted his feelings. "Remember when I told you about how I got the runes, the guy who sold them to me?"

"Right, Aja the Deal Maker. I'm still amazed that you met him," Bart said.

"I usually get feelings about people. Take Amal, he was

selling junk too. I got the feeling that he was a nice guy. He didn't have anything I wanted, but I knew he wouldn't cheat me. And Pierre, he sold clocks, and I knew I could trust him too. But Kassandra, she was only interested in selling her old cups."

Bart guffawed. "You've met the Water Lady?"

Sammy nodded. "She was beautiful. That was about two years ago. I was still a little kid then. She couldn't affect me then like she could now."

"Why, I've heard her beauty is beyond measure. They say Helen of Troy, she is, face that launched a thousand ships and all that."

"She was attractive, and I was drawn to her in a childish way, but she wasn't interested in talking. No good vibes at all."

Bart walked ahead, leading Sammy through the last few remaining doors. "A woman as old and beautiful as she, I'd wager there's more to her wares than cups."

Sammy removed the Berkana rune from his bracelet. "Like I was saying about the runes, I think they're special in some way." He considered what his heart told him to do.

"I'll wager they're ancient and quite valuable," Bart said.

Sammy rubbed the rune between his thumb and forefinger, catching the edge on his thumbnail, something he did when he was nervous. He needed to be sure. Besides Elizabeth, the runes were one of the few things he really cared about.

Sammy paused before stepping through an ancient crumbling door marked with hieroglyphs. "Bart, take it."

Bart looked back from the other side of the door with a puzzled look on his face. Sammy held out his hand, palm up, the rune glimmering in the low light. Bart blinked, his jaw dropping low.

Seeing that Bart wasn't interested in the gift, Sammy dropped his hand and continued on through the sandy door. He'd never given anyone a real gift before, never had anything of worth to give. He was confused why Bart didn't take it. Bart had only shown poor manners up until that point, so nothing had changed. "If you didn't want it, you could just say 'no thanks' and keep going instead of standing there like a bozo. We've got to keep moving."

Bart pointed at the rune in Sammy's hand. "No, bloke. Your runes, they passed through the doors."

Sammy shrugged. The wheels in his head turned. "Yeah, I've been wearing them the whole time."

"They are magic then, and powerful at that," Bart said.

Sammy swelled at the idea of owning something special. He'd never owned anything more valuable than a few pairs of khakis and a few school shirts. "Yeah?"

"They come through the maze. Only truly powerful craft work artifacts could make it through, like my compass. The prison keeps most craft work trinkets out. I'd assumed they'd been transported already, back to the altar."

"Why would they be on the altar?" Sammy asked.

"It's where the prison sends them when they disappear from our pockets," Bart said. "Had one bloke accuse me of stealing his infinite bag. Had a terrible time convincing him it was back at the start. He nearly took my head off."

"Well, take it. We're in this together," Sammy said.

Bart took the rune and tied it around his neck with a shoelace he pulled from his pocket. "Thank you. It's kind of you to offer something like that. I won't hold you to it, though. If you change your mind and want it back later, I won't think any less of you."

Sammy laughed. "I won't ask for it back." He felt good about giving Bart the rune. It was the right thing to do.

Bart stuck out his hand. "This makes us proper accomplices now."

Sammy shook it. "The two amigos."

"We're at the bottom. Just one last door," Bart said. "Before..."

Sammy grabbed the rings on either side of the towering cathedral doors and pulled them open. Red flames rushed out at them. Sammy jumped back, but not quickly enough. The flames scorched his skin and clothing. Some of the hair at the front of his head shriveled up and fell away.

Sammy patted his smoldering clothes. "Ouch." The smell of burnt hair stuck in his nose.

Bart was unharmed. "Mr. Impatient. We gotta learn you some protection wards if you gonna keep opening doors all willy-nilly as such." He pointed at the door. "In you go."

Sammy snorted and shook his head, incredulous. "You want me to go into the fire?"

"Go on. It'll be fine... so long as you don't tarry about," Bart said.

Sammy seethed before jumping headlong into the fire. He immediately regretted it.

18

THE COUNCIL

The Council of Protection convened in the Hall of Knowing, in deep space, among the stars, outside of time. They sat behind invisible tables in unseen chairs arranged in a circle. To the average Earthenite, it would appear as if they were levitating.

Lord Durga stood at the center of the wide circle, hands clasped at the waist, a wide grin across his classically handsome face. A gold pendant hung from his thick necklace. The feoh symbol resembled the modern English lower case F. The glint of silver threading woven through his fine black waistcoat sparkled like the gleaming white teeth behind his wry smile.

A thin, tall elderly man in long white robes rose and addressed the council. "Respected members of the council, I bring before you one of Earth's most heinous villains. We know him as Lord Durga, the Slave Maker. How old he is or when he began on his path of horrors, we do not know. His given name is lost to us. He has eluded this council for centuries. His path of destruction has cut wide and deep.

There is no lack of evidence of his malice and hatred for the people of Earth."

"Honorable Erland Skuld, this Council of Protection is well aware of Lord Durga's doings. We should do right to proceed and bring forth the evidence." Intensity burned in Mr. Tesla's dark, deep-set eyes.

"Yes, Honorable Mr. Tesla, a wise suggestion. Esteemed members of the council, I present to you the evidence brought forth by myself, Erland Skuld, for the purpose of prosecution of Durga, charged with viciously enslaving the peoples of Earth for profit."

Erland Skuld raised his right hand, activating the images that appeared above Lord Durga's head. The first to appear was that of a man and woman dressed in animal skins. Their body odor was quite potent. Some of the council members placed fingers to their noses to block the pungent stench. The man and woman in the viewer let out fierce war screams. With wooden clubs raised above their heads, they charged into a simple camp composed of a man and a woman nursing an infant. After the successful raid, they lumbered back to their cave, carrying the child with them.

More images flashed across the space. The next image to appear was of several men and women clad in thick iron chains. The captives stood on a wooden platform while sweaty old men discussed their value.

Lord Durga appeared in some of the images, often smiling and laughing, very aware of the pain he had orchestrated. The smell of blood filled the open space.

"As you can see from the evidence, Durga has shown no remorse. He shows only hatred and malice. His lust for power and wealth has led to the enslavement of the Earth's people."

Erland Skuld paced, his intent blue eyes locked on the

accused. The Slave Maker held his gaze. Fury smoldered in the blackness of the prisoner's pupils. The mutterings and nods of agreement quieted as Erland Skuld resumed.

"What may have been a lush paradise has now become a world ensnared with avarice and pain. Left unguided, the people of Earth would have grown into a caring and gentle race. He has poisoned their hearts. They have been molded in his image. They have become what he made them, cold and greedy. The average twenty-first-century Earthenites care little for one another or even for their own home. They wantonly pollute the Earth for financial gain. Some barter their own children into bondage. This is Lord Durga's doing. He has taught them to covet their goods. They hoard the plentiful nourishment the Earth gives freely. The gluttonous few gorge while the many feeble waste away."

Erland Skuld paused. Scenes of barefoot children sifting through pale-brown sand and chipping away at jagged gray rock flashed across the open space. "They value his money so highly; they are willing to mold each other into it. They see each other only as currency, only as a means to an end. The Earthenites have lost the ability to see each other as they see themselves, as complete beings, one with the universe.

"Durga has done well in concealing his corruption. He's hidden behind lesser men, controlling and shaping from the shadows, manipulating others into acting on his will. He would say to one chieftain, 'That other chief has more than you. You should take it from him.' He would say to political leaders, 'They are not men. They are not civil like us. They are heathen, cattle. They do not have the right to freedom as we do. You should enslave them, make them work your land. You will be rich.' He would say to the leaders, 'The land is not theirs. The land is yours. Take it. The Earth is a resource to be mined and sold for profit.'"

Erland Skuld stood and faced the council, his arms folded across his chest.

"They maim and kill each other. They enslave each other. They bleed the Earth of its life... for profit. They do so on his word, at his instruction."

Lord Durga raged, spitting every word with the snapping jaws of a feral beast. "Was it not I who gave the Earthenites order where there was only chaos? Did I not give them the gift of rule, of laws? Yes, I guided them as children while you watched from your high tower, indifferent, consumed by your own ambitions. I brought them into the light while you did nothing, and you stand in judgment of me?"

Durga shook his head. "You cannot hold me. This little show of yours will not last. I will be free again, and when I am, you will pay. My magic is stronger than your hope, your charity." He pointed at one of the council members, a calm, elderly bald-headed man. "You, Mahatma Gandhi, you gave your life at my hand. What has your peace gained you? Only death."

Gandhi only looked on with pity.

He pointed at others, the seething words dripping from his curled lips. "You will all do the same. I will tear down this house and build my own. I will build my house of strength upon your rubble and ash."

"No, you will not," Erland Skuld said. "This council has agreed upon the sentence of life imprisonment, however long that may last."

"Imprison me? Your council's vanity is astounding. You think you can imprison me, the greatest wizard the Earth has ever known? Your prisons are a pittance before me."

"Quite correct, we've yet to erect a penitentiary that can

hold one such as yourself," Erland Skuld said. "Nevertheless, you've been sentenced to a lifetime's imprisonment within the shadow realm, in the prison you yourself have created. You'll be housed in the very same dungeon that once held your enemies. The tables have turned, and those who were once your victims will now be your jailers. Those tools which aided you in gaining so much influence will join you in your imprisonment. Those Morsels of Desire, that Shackle of Bondage, and Lead of the Death March, they shall be locked away and will never again see the light of day."

19

A COOL DRINK

Sammy landed with a thud. His side hurt from the impact, but the fire hurt more. He rolled around in the dirt, smothering his smoldering clothing. He batted at his clothes until they stopped smoking. Bart helped.

THEY WERE IN A CAVE, round and high, only thirty feet in diameter. The cathedral doors were gone, just as Sammy had expected.

IN THE MIDDLE of the round room was a pool of water. A white light glowed from far beneath the surface.

The shimmering water sparkled, calling to him. Sammy was incredibly thirsty, his tongue swollen in his mouth. He needed to drink. He scrambled over to the pool, scooped up some of the water, and brought it to his mouth.

. . .

BART SLAPPED Sammy's hand away before he could drink in the cool, delicious water.

"WHAT THE HECK?" Sammy swabbed his scorched forehead with his wet hand. The coolness soothed his hot skin.

"ARE YOU DAFT OR JUST STUPID?" Bart asked.

SAMMY SCOOPED up another handful of the cool water. "I'm thirsty."

BART SLAPPED HIS HAND AGAIN. "Stop it."

"GET AWAY FROM ME," Sammy said. He needed to drink the water. He couldn't not drink the water. He remembered Elizabeth and her frantic attack on the steak, and yet he still wanted to drink. He plunged his hand into the refreshing goodness and scooped up a mouthful. It effervesced, going down his throat like an antacid.

BART GABBED SAMMY by the shirt and dragged him to the side, away from the glowing pool.

"GET—" Sammy tried to speak, but Bart shoved something uncomfortably large into his mouth, about the size of a twenty-five-cent gumball. Sammy tried spitting it out, but Bart held his mouth shut. It tasted like dirt.

SAMMY FLAILED his arms and slapped at Bart, but he couldn't get the bigger boy off him. He hated Bart. He needed to drink. Sammy bashed Bart on the head and face with his fists, but Bart wouldn't let up. Sammy swallowed then fell unconscious. He dreamt of a scary man yelling at him to "don't drink the water."

SAMMY'S HEAD ACHED. The thought of water repulsed him. He gagged and opened his eyes. The light from the pool hurt his eyes. Bart sat on the ground, staring at him.

"WHAT HAPPENED? How long was I out for?" Sammy asked.

"YOU JUST ABOUT KILLED YOURSELF," Bart said. "You'd have managed if I hadn't forced a medicine pill down your throat. Don't worry. You were only out for a few minutes."

"Is that what gave me this headache?"

"AFRAID SO. Don't have much access to magical components here in the prison, and I don't get out much. Gotta make do with what I have available. Good thing I had a spare pill on me, or you'd be a goner. I make 'em in my spare time and try to keep a few on hand. Never know what could happen down here."

"You gave me bootleg magical medication?" Sammy asked.

"You could say that. I didn't have a proper toadstool for the pill, so I used one of the local fungi that grow here in the prison. Did the job, though, and your banging head will be good as new, quick enough."

"But what happened?" Sammy asked.

Bart lifted a stone and looked under it. "You drank the delicious poison water."

A deep, scratchy voice whispered in their ears. "Lead of movement. Shackles of will. Morsel of hunger."

"Who said that?" Sammy said.

"It's the prison, warning us."

"Then ask it to help us."

. . .

Bart shook his head. "It don't converse properly. Hear it in my dreams sometimes."

Sammy gave Bart a puzzled look. "Did it ever mention Elizabeth?"

"No, it didn't never talk of your pup, but I think I've seen those things it mentioned just now," Bart said.

"What are they?"

Bart got on his knees and dug a hole, pushing the stony earth away with his hands. He dug about a foot down then got back up and dusted himself off. "He talked about a lead, like a leash. Master had a leather leash. I seen it once or twice around some guests' necks. Thought it strange the gentry and nobles should wear a leash. What's more strange was the look in their eye. It was all glazed over, like they were in a trance or something."

"Wait. Your master had one of these things? Wha—"

"That's what I said. And he had a shackle too," Bart said. "I seen it once in a glass case. I thought it was a souvenir from his days with the East India Trading Company."

. . .

SAMMY SHOT BART A SIDELONG GLANCE. "Your master worked with the East India Trading Company? What kind of horrible person did you work for?" He had a suspicion that Bart was more than just the caretaker.

BART RAN his hands all along the cavern walls as if he was feeling for something. "Listen up, this is important. The morsels, I seen lots of times. He had a gold tray, always covered. None of the servants were permitted to touch it. Never. I seen one housemaid get close with her feather duster, and the master flew into a rage. She was gone the following day. No one heard from her again."

SAMMY MIMICKED Bart and searched the walls. He didn't know what he was looking for, but he would know if he found it. "The morsels, what did they do?"

"HE HAD lots of tricks to make people do what he wanted, but he used the tray often. It seemed easier. No potions to brew, no incantations, just hand them a chocolate. Who don't like chocolate? I never had any myself. Master had other levers for me."

"AND THEY DID WHAT HE WANTED?" Sammy asked.

"NOT RIGHT AWAY, always. Some people resisted, but I could tell they wanted more of them chocolates. Their eyes flittered back and forth to the tray. Sometimes, they'd storm off.

Master got a laugh out of that. The funny thing was they'd be back the next day for sure, dying to get another bite of them candies. I think it had to do with how much they ate. A small person only required a nibble. A bigger person needed a piece or two."

"Sounds like Elizabeth and the steak, me and the water," Sammy said. "But if your master used the same tools, you know how to beat them."

"I said I seen 'em. I didn't say I knew what to do," Bart said.

Sammy snorted.

Bart looked at the ground and spat, his face sullen. "He didn't trust me, never told me nothing important. Only told me what I needed to know to get his jobs done, do his dirty work."

"How did you get to be caretaker anyway?" Sammy asked.

Bart examined the ceiling. "Enough of that. We gotta find our way out of this room."

"I thought you knew how to get out. Isn't that what you've

been looking for? The key hidden under a rock or something?"

"THIS IS AS FAR as anyone's ever gotten," Bart said. "I only known about the poison water 'cause I saw a bloke take a drink then run around in circles like a madman. Ran himself silly."

"BUT YOU'RE THE CARETAKER," Sammy said. "How don't you know about the prison if you're the caretaker?"

"IT'S MORE complicated than all that, but right now, we've got to find our way through this room."

"THERE'S nothing here except the pool. It has to be the pool."

"THE WATER'S POISON," Bart said. "We can't go in there."

"THEN WHY IS THERE a light at the bottom?" Sammy said.

"I DON'T KNOW. To light the room?"

SAMMY ROLLED HIS EYES. "Lights always mean go. Lighthouses, the light at the end of the tunnel, get it?"

· · ·

"I GET IT, but I can't swim," Bart said. "I tried once. Besides, that's no shallow puddle. It's at least twenty feet deep."

"IF I SWALLOW any more water, just give me another medicine ball." Sammy filled his lungs and held his breath. He'd tried swimming once before too. It hadn't turned out well. This time had to be different. Elizabeth was counting on him. He focused on the white light at the bottom of the pool and jumped in headfirst, like he'd seen divers do on television.

THE SPLASH WAS DEAFENING. The water filled his ears and nose. He kicked frantically. He pushed the water with his hands. It worked. He swam toward the light. He was great for a moment, then his lungs felt uncomfortable. The discomfort turned into pain. His lungs ached. The light was so close, but out of reach. Was it moving away from him? Every time he was close enough to touch the white ball of light, it seemed to move just out of reach. He kicked hard. It didn't help. He'd failed. The pain in his lungs subsided, and his eyes closed.

20

———

THE KIPPER AND THE CELL

Bart propped Sammy up. He pounded on Sammy's back. Nothing. He pounded harder. Nothing. He laid Sammy on his side and pounded again. Still nothing.

"Blast it, Sammy, wake up." If only Bart had some magic, some incantation or potion that drained the water from Sammy's lungs. But he didn't.

Bart had no idea how long Sammy had been under. He had only just woken up himself. Time could have stretched. That blasted prison and its time games.

Bart needed magic. Maybe the runes would help. They were quite powerful, or the prison would have sent them back to the altar room. Bart took the rune from around his neck and placed it in his hand. He slammed the rune into Sammy's back. Maybe that would get the water out. He slammed again and again. Sammy sputtered. It worked. Bart slammed the rune against Sammy's back once more for good measure.

Sammy coughed. "Ouch."

Bart fell to the ground, soaking wet and coughing. Water

dribbled from his mouth. He spat out the foul, putrid poison. It tasted like spinach. He hated spinach. He thanked the wonders it didn't get into his belly, or he would have been a goner. He kissed his rune and hung it around his neck once more.

Sammy lay there, coughing and hurling. At least he was alive. If he hadn't been, Bart would've killed him.

"What the devil was that?" Bart asked. "I told you I couldn't swim, and you jump in anyway?"

Sammy gagged.

"Lucky I saw you at the bottom, wiggling around like a little kipper caught on a line. If I hadn't jumped in after, you'd be dead as a doornail."

Sammy coughed.

"And where do you get off jumping into magical pools anyhow? I told you it was poison, didn't I?"

"Thanks." Sammy coughed more.

"All right. Get it all out, you daft nutter. Be quick about it."

They were in a stone room, about four square feet. The bitter taste of the water mixed with a moldy, musty stench that stuck in their noses. Other than their dripping clothes, there was no sign of the pool or the cave. The room was empty except for an ancient straw-covered cot and a tall, thin rectangular window. An open cell door welcomed them, the cold bars covered in rust.

"Oh, god. We're here, aren't we?" Bart asked. "In the prison proper?"

Sammy still choked up bitter water.

Dark brownish-red stains spotted the cold stone floor. Bart peeked through the cell door. He saw only a corridor of cells. "Come on, then. We ain't safe." He dug through the straw and found a piece of ancient, yellowed parchment.

"Saw it in a dream once. Thought I might find it there." Bart pulled his compass from his pocket and held it up to the parchment, which detailed the layout of the prison.

"What's that?" Sammy asked.

"You alive, then?" Bart shot him a sidelong glance. "A little thirsty, were you?"

"It worked, didn't it?" Sammy asked.

"That's right," Bart said. "We got through the pool. No thanks to you. The rune saved you."

"You saved me. The rune only helped. Now show me what you found."

Bart pointed to a spot on the parchment. "It's a map of sorts. See there? It's marked 'morsels.' We'll need them, like the council said."

"But weren't we following your compass?"

"But my compass don't show the path, only the direction to the man. With some luck, we'll catch up to Culty before he gets to Durga."

"Wait," Sammy said. "Where are we?"

"That's the rough part. We're in the prison proper. See this here? It says 'inmates.'" Bart pointed to their location on the map. "I'll bet them inmates got something to do with the shackle or something."

"Inmates? I thought it was a prison for just Lord Durga."

"We're going to find out, aren't we?"

"Did the cop come through here?" Sammy asked. "How come he didn't find the map?"

"Don't know. The floor was dry other than the mess we made. And the map wasn't hidden very well. Either he's on a different route, or he's too daft to look under the cushions. The prison may be toying with us. It does things like that, the little whispers and the dreams. I'll wager it enjoys playing god, revealing just enough. Let's press on, but slowly. No more rushing about. This is dangerous business."

"Can't you do the aura thing again?" Sammy asked.

"It don't work like that. Auras are useful for learning intention, but not as a tracking tool. They dissipate too quickly. It ain't a breadcrumb trail." Bart stepped through the cell door into the corridor.

21

THE GUILTY PLEA

Bart hung his head, surrounded by the huge circle of elders. The elders levitated. Their eyes studied his every move. There was no floor or ceiling, only floating tables and chairs. Their craft work was beyond Bart's comprehension. Beyond the circle was only the blackness of open space in every direction.

His world had spun out of control. How had it come to this? Everything was all so much bigger than he'd ever imagined. The universe was so much bigger. He thought the master had it all under control. Sure, he was the master's footstool, but everyone else was his.

Bart had sailed the globe. Nothing was off limits. He got what he wanted, when he wanted. Now he just wanted to go back to the street, where it had been simple and safe. Sure, he'd taken some lumps, but at least he'd been able to sleep at night. This was incomprehensible.

"Mr. Baker, what have you to say for your actions?" asked a man in blue robes with a red beard. "How do you plead?"

"Guilty, Your Hon... Majes... I followed the man, did all

107

he asked. Horrible things, I done," Bart said. "I expect no mercy from the court. I deserve none. I suppose I could use some time to myself to reflect on what I done."

Images appeared in the space over where Bart stood. He saw himself, so long ago, thin and ragged, when he had still been himself.

A white-bearded gentleman in long white robes stood and addressed Bart. "Do you recognize this boy?"

The image above Bart's head moved. It was him, on his knees, pulling weeds from a bed of cabbages. The pale-gray dirt was more dust than soil. It stuck to the sweat dripping down his brow.

"I do, sir. That's me when I was just a pup."

"And what are you doing here?" the man asked.

"Sir, that's me helping old Mrs. Murphy with her vegetable garden," Bart said. "Her hands couldn't work the soil."

He remembered that day so long ago. The hot summer sun had beaten down on him, burning his skin. The wooden handle of the pickax splintered and bit into him. The blisters bubbled up and popped open in a cycle, leaving his hands red and raw. That night, his face, neck, and palms burned with a fury, but he had drifted into slumber without a care in the world.

"And what is this?" the man asked.

The image changed. Bart had a smaller boy in his arms. The boy screamed and writhed in agony. His thigh was covered in black and red burns.

Bart snorted and massaged his elbow. He recalled the smell of charcoal and roasted meat. His arms had ached for days afterward. "That's me carrying little Billy Flannigan. He burnt his leg with the forge. I took him home to his mum."

"And why did you do that?" the man asked. "Was it your responsibility? Was it not the work of the smith to care for his damaged apprentice?"

Bart looked away. "What else could I do? The boy was in pain. That's all the reason I needed."

The bearded man drummed his fingers on the table. "You took no reward for your work in carrying Billy home. Ten miles as the crow flies, was it not? The boy's mother offered you stew. You refused even though you yourself faced the looming threat of starvation."

"Billy's father passed on, season before," Bart said. "They come on rough times. I could eat without taking food from their mouths, little baby and all."

The man tapped the table harder, louder. "You could eat? And yet your bones tell another tale, crying out for sustenance from behind those oversized rags."

"I didn't like thieving. I had to when it came too much to bear, when I thought I'd die if I didn't get a bite. I didn't take much, just enough to get me by."

The man stroked his white beard and slammed a hand down onto the wood. "Just enough, you say?"

"Sir, please don't. I can't take any more. The one don't have nothing to do with the other. I plead guilty. Make your judgment and be done with it. I done wrong, and I want to pay. I can't undo what I done, but I need to make it right with myself."

The man held up a hand. Bart looked down past his feet to the infinite below. The Earth looked calm from so far away, blue, round, and peaceful. The stars twinkled under him. It could have been different.

The whole council erupted into a flurry of hushed whispers. They conversed, consulting with one another, some slamming their hands down onto the impossibly long table. Bart winced at the sound. Finally, the whispers quieted, and the elders settled.

"You yourself have seen Durga's deeds, firsthand," the man said. "You've seen the evidence put forth by this council. You know the damage he's done."

"I do, sir," Bart said.

"You've made no case in your own defense." The man looked at him thoughtfully. "Why is that?"

"I done bad things. I poisoned a man."

"We are well aware of your actions and have also considered your renunciation of your position in Durga's employ. You had no idea that you'd be standing here, that you were under our eye, and yet you chose to leave. More precisely, you attempted to leave your dreaded master, well aware of the dangers in doing so. Bartholomew, you're a victim, one of many. History is full of great men abusing the need of the poor and uneducated."

"He didn't take very kindly to my departure," Bart said. "I thought I was safe in Morocco until I wasn't. My reeducation, it was a burden, but I bore it."

"We are in a very precarious position," the man said. "You've come to learn many very old and very dangerous skills. Should we let you back into the world, you may be tempted to use your considerable talents in ways that some might find distasteful."

"I understand, sir. You'd do right to keep me locked away, unable to hurt anyone ever again."

The man exhaled a long, slow breath, his eyes filled with pity. "But we feel it would be an injustice to withhold your freedom. You didn't choose to commit those atrocities. In most cases, you had no idea of what you were doing. At worst, you were only slightly culpable, a minor accomplice.

At best, merely a tool without complicity. But I urge you, choose your friends more wisely in the future. Your talents, you've earned those through hard lessons. Keep them well and heed the words of this council. We'll be watching."

"I aim to make things right, sir," Bart said.

22

INMATES

"We've got to find the Shackle and the leash or whatever, to get Elizabeth back," Sammy said.

"I'm glad you've been paying attention," Bart said.

Sammy breathed deeply, silently reciting his mantra. *When the fear passes, only I'll remain.* "I'm a little stressed out. Cut me some slack."

"Come on." Bart snuck down the passageway.

Sammy followed Bart down the torchlit corridor. The stone walls perspired. The drips echoed in Sammy's ears like an off-beat clock. Skeletons lay about, lining the hall, shadows catching in their eye sockets. Dingy black-and-white clothing hung from the bones.

"Who are these blokes, then?" Bart asked under his breath.

"They've been dead a long time," Sammy said. "They're only bone and cloth, nothing else left."

"And those hammers in their hands."

Sammy's skin crawled. The sound of a hundred angry men erupted from around a corner. "What's that?"

Bart said, "I don't know," then turned a corner.

"It's loud, like school at lunchtime," Sammy said.

"This ain't school, but it's mealtime for sure."

Sammy turned the corner into a massive hall of tables and filthy, hairy men. They wore similar black-and-gray-striped clothing.

Sammy grabbed Bart and hurled him back around the corner. "Hide before they see us."

Sammy closed his eyes and recounted what he saw. They were prisoners, they were fighting, and there were a lot of them.

"Did you see that bloke yanking at that other chap's ear?" Bart asked.

Sammy peeked around the corner. "No, I saw two guys head-butting each other like the rams in a nature magazine."

Bart pulled him back by his shirt. "What are you doing? You trying to get us killed?"

Sammy grabbed the map and studied it. "We got to get around them. There're cells on the other side. It's the way through."

"And how do you suggest we get by those lunatics without getting ground into mincemeat ourselves?"

"They didn't even notice us. We can just sneak by."

"You are a nutter," Bart said. "Did you see the size of them maniacs, and what they were doing to each other?"

Sammy bent down and removed the clothing from a nearby skeleton. "We can do this. We have to."

"Disguises?" Bart asked incredulously. "You want to play dress-up now?"

Sammy pulled on the skeleton's prisoner outfit. "It's the only way." The cloth was rough, like canvas. It smelled like a forgotten loaf of white bread that had been allowed to grow green and fuzzy.

Bart undressed another nearby skeleton and slipped on its uniform. "Humph."

"How do I look? Like a proper convict?" Bart hunched his shoulders and hung his head low. "Saw a few shorter blokes in there. We might could fit in if we're lucky enough."

"It'll have to do. Make straight for the other side." Sammy stepped around the corner and headed straight for the crowd of angry prisoners. He kept his eyes on the ground as he entered the crowd. It worked. They didn't even notice him.

It was like a bumper car ride. He was slammed on all sides. A mangled man fell onto him, knocking him over, but he regained his footing and continued. The prisoners punched and kicked and beat each other with a ferocity he'd never seen or imagined. The screams and howls drowned out every other sound.

He was halfway to the hall. Where was Bart? He looked back for his friend and exhaled. Bart was only half a pace behind him.

A dark-mustached, barrel-chested prisoner stepped in Sammy's path. With fury in his eyes, he pointed a thick, menacing finger at Sammy. "You! You've got it! Where is it? Give it to me!" the prisoner demanded.

"Oh no," Sammy said.

The fighting stopped. The hall grew silent, and the prisoners turned their attention to Sammy.

A prisoner with too-long fingernails grabbed Sammy by the arm, cutting into the skin. "He's the one. He's got it!"

His heart felt as if it was going to pump out of his chest. "No, I don't have it!"

"Where is it? Where is it?" the crowd demanded in unison.

A million filthy hands grabbed at him. They took him by the arms and legs and held him up high over the crowd.

Where are they taking me? No. No. No. No. No. No No. This can't be happening.

"Use the rune!" Bart yelled. "G—" Bart's voice stopped abruptly as if the wind had been knocked out of him mid-word.

Sammy squirmed and writhed and wiggled his arms free. He pulled the rune from his bracelet and smacked the prisoner who had him on the right shoulder. The prisoner flew onto his back. Sammy flailed his arms, sending prisoners flying in all directions. He fell to the stone floor, hitting his head. Blood dripped into his eyes.

Bart was only ten feet away, surrounded by the furious inmates. They had him by the wrists and ankles.

A tall inmate stood before him with a broken table leg in his hand. The inmate pointed the table leg at Bart. "Where is it?"

Sammy ran and jumped, smashing his rune into the tall prisoner's back with all his might.

The prisoner flew into Bart, knocking heads and sending the whole group to the floor. The room burst into pandemonium.

Sammy grabbed Bart by the arm and dragged his limp body to the end of the hall. Looking back, he saw the inmates had lost track of them in the commotion and resumed their search for whatever it was they looked for. A few fights had broken out between some of the unrulier prisoners.

Sammy dragged Bart's body around a corner into the far corridor, which was also lined with cells. Each had one bunk and one window, nothing more. He pulled Bart into one of the cells and slapped him across the face once, then again. "Wake up. Wake up." He slapped Bart with the hand holding the rune.

Bart stirred. "What the devil are you doing? Get your grubby arse away from me." Bart sat up, massaging his cheek.

Sammy examined Bart's head. "I thought you were dead." Bart had several severe-looking bumps, and a trickle of blood fell from his right ear.

"By the look of your melon, you got it worse than I did." Bart pointed at the blood dripping from Sammy's crown.

Sammy's head did hurt, but he worked through the pain. He had to. He ripped the sleeve from his shirt and tied it around his wounded head then tore the other sleeve and wrapped it around Bart's ear.

"Well, look at you, Doctor Nichols. I say we just rub some dirt on it and be off." Bart tried to stand but fell back with a thud.

"Take a minute. We're hidden, for now." Sammy ripped his leather bracelet and used the leather to wrap the rune to his finger. "Just in case they find us, and we have to defend ourselves."

Sammy wrenched Bart's clutched fist open and tied Bart's rune to his finger with the shoelace.

"Thanks for telling me to use the rune. I thought I was done for. It's better as a ring, in case we have to hit someone, like those maniacs back there."

"They focus the will, magical magnifiers..." Bart said before he began to nod off.

Sammy slapped him. "Wake up."

"All right, governor." Bart slurred, barely able to speak. "No violence, we said."

No. No. I can't lose two friends. Bart can't die.

Sammy rifled through Bart's pockets. He found shoelaces, buttons, sticks, and stones.

Where? Where? Where? Where?

In the breast pocket of Bart's jacket, Sammy found two pills, the size of gumballs.

One of these has to do something.

The first was dark brown, the color of bitter chocolate. The second was beige, like cafe con leche from the bodega.

He bobbed them up and down, feeling their weight. They felt the same. He smelled the dark pill. It smelled like dirt. He smelled the second. It smelled like... mushrooms.

Sammy jammed the mushroom pill into Bart's open mouth. "Come on. Chew."

He checked for a pulse. Nothing. He put his cheek next to Bart's nose. No breath. Sammy hung his head. Bart was dead.

Sammy sat with Bart for a moment, considering his next step. He stared at the ring wrapped to Bart's colorless finger and folded Bart's hands on his lap. "You keep that. You might need it on the other side, for all that karmic debt. Goodbye, friend."

He hoisted himself from the floor and examined the other cells that lined the corridor. He flipped over every straw mattress and checked every wall and floor for loose stones.

None of the prisoners had come around the corner into the corridor. Maybe they'd forgotten about him. He heard them fighting again. The screams echoed off the walls. He checked dozens of cells. None held any way of escape. He finally reached the last cell at the end of the corridor.

The last cell was the same, except for one important detail. On the floor, in the corner, was a gleaming white dinner plate. It held the most rancid, putrid substance

Sammy had ever smelled. He retched and emptied his stomach of its bile.

It's the plate. It's the same plate.

He picked up the plate of putrid goop. It changed. The goop vanished, and the steak and fries appeared. It smelled amazing. He dropped it, and it fell to the floor. But the plate didn't shatter. It sat on the floor, full of putrid goop.

Sammy remembered the whispering advice from earlier. "The morsels."

Sammy picked up the plate again. The steak appeared again. It smelled delicious. He was so hungry. He brought the plate up to his nose, inhaling the seared beef. *Just a taste,* he thought.

He dropped the plate. *It's not real.*

Picking up the plate once more, the goop turned to steak and fries again. He walked out of the cell. The goop returned. The steak was gone. *What the...*

He went back into the cell. The steak's wonderful aroma wafted up to Sammy's nose again. He flipped the mattress, pushing and prodding every stone in the cell. None came loose. *What am I supposed to do? This makes no sense.*

Everything in that place had been a puzzle so far. But this one was the most dangerous. The prisoners had killed Bart already. Sammy didn't want to be next. *You swim in water. You walk through doors. What do you do in a cell? Nothing, that's it.* He closed the cell door. The click of the lock echoed in his ears.

He placed the plate back down on the stone floor, in the corner where he found it. He felt defeated. Not only was he a prisoner, but he had shut himself in a cell with food that would drive him mad. It couldn't have gotten any worse. He placed the straw mattress back onto the cot and sat down. His eyes flitted back to the steak that smelled so good.

The noise and commotion from the mess hall got a little louder, but he didn't care. *Let them do what they want.* Sleep might help him forget about Bart and about Elizabeth. Maybe Sammy could sleep until the end came. He laid his head back and closed his eyes. He heard a click, then another.

He jumped up from the bed. The cell door was slightly ajar. He looked around, but he was alone. Who could have unlocked the door? Then, a rectangular outline appeared in the stone wall. He pushed on the wall. The stones came apart, and the door opened into darkness.

It was the way through. He could escape, but he had to check on Bart one last time. He pulled the bunk into the dark opening in the stone wall. If a phone book in the door of his building kept him from getting locked out, a cot would work too. It was only magic.

He pulled the dingy mattress halfway through the cell door and left it there like a phone book. He hoped the cell wouldn't shut him out. He picked up the gleaming white plate, barely able to resist the aroma of the fine seared steak. If that magical steak worked anything like the chocolates Bart talked about, it might be useful in some way.

He started back down the corridor toward the mess hall. Bart was gone. Someone had stolen his body. "Dang it." He had to find Bart's body and find the rune. Who knew what these horrible prisoners might do. Bart didn't deserve that.

Sammy turned the corner into the mess hall. The inmates all stopped and stared, frozen.

I hope this works. "Inmates, your food," Sammy yelled, placing the gleaming of plate of steak frites on the nearest table and backing away slowly.

The prisoners ran to the food. They grabbed at the food, fries flying everywhere. They climbed over each other to get at the plate. As more and more prisoners got a taste, they calmed and passed the plate around. The steak was still on the plate. Each prisoner had a handful of steak and fries, but the plate was full, like the fish and loaves of bread from the stories at church.

It went on for ten minutes. Yells of laughter filled the hall. Sammy used the time to search the mess hall, checking every inch of it for Bart, but Bart wasn't there. When the prisoners had their fill, a greasy-faced man put the plate on the center table of the hall. They all stood and faced Sammy, waiting.

"Hello." Sammy waved, hoping the steak had worked like the chocolate in Bart's story.

The prisoners laughed and slapped each other's backs.

"If you're taking orders, I'll have what they're having."

Sammy jumped out of his skin. He turned and saw Bart standing there. He was alive. The bumps on his head were gone.

Sammy shook his head. He couldn't believe his eyes. "You're... you're alive?"

Bart nodded and massaged his temples. "Dead men don't have headaches like the one I got."

"Where'd you go? I thought they took you."

Bart shrugged. "I woke up, and you were gone. I went searching for ya."

Sammy furrowed his brow. "Searching? Where? I was down the hall."

"Went back into the crowd," Bart said. "Thought they had you prisoner."

Sammy pointed, amazed. "You went back in? That's crazy."

"No big to do with my new ring. I shoved them blokes aside like children. They caught on quick enough and made way. I heard of these runes growing in power. Good thing it kicked in when it did. And what have you been up to? Looks like you've got a captive audience, so to speak."

"The inmates of insanity are at your command." The cool breeze whispered in their ears.

"You hear that? At your command," Bart said.

Sammy turned to the crowd. It was a strange new feeling. He'd never been in charge before. It was a little unsettling.

The tallest and widest of the inmates pushed through to the front. "Your orders, sir?"

My orders? Sammy walked to the plate in the middle of the crowd and grabbed a steak from it then went over to the huge inmate. "We'll need help later."

"I am Edmond. Call, and we'll come."

"Thanks, Edmond. I'll call. Trust me."

Sammy removed the remains of his prisoner shirt and wrapped the steak in it, tying it to his torso like a sling. He might need it later. When he had it secured, he looked at Bart. "Ready to get out of here?"

"Elizabeth's waiting," Bart said.

They walked to the door in the stone wall.

Bart's eyes opened wide. "You been busy, I see. Looks like you might have this whole magical adventure thing all worked out. Our little man's all grown up. Tell me all about it later. Our Elizabeth's waiting."

They stepped through the darkness.

23

CHASING STONES

The doorway from the prison vanished. They stood on a circular stone platform. It was black and shiny, standing about a foot high and ten feet in diameter. Statues of armored knights with swords drawn surrounded them, just a few feet from the raised platform. There was no sign that Culty or Elizabeth had been through there.

"What's this, then?" Bart said, his words echoing.

Sammy pointed to one of the knights. "They don't look friendly."

Bart nodded. "I imagine they aren't accustomed to having guests."

Sammy looked between the knights and saw rows and rows of similar statues lined up in neat groups all around them.

Torches lined the high walls far off in the distance. The next set of statues stood about twenty feet away and looked the same as those just outside the platform. Farther in the distance stood statues of soldiers on horseback. Others, even farther, were archers.

Sammy gazed into the distance. "They're everywhere."

"Thousands, I'd wager," Bart said

Sammy moved closer to one of the swords. "No way we can disguise ourselves as one of these. They're ten feet tall."

"Don't touch it. We don't know their nature." Bart reached out to grab Sammy's arm, but Sammy had already retracted his hand.

"We can't stay here forever," Sammy said. "We've got to get going."

Bart examined his map and compass. "The questions is: which way. Like you said, they're everywhere."

Sammy crept closer to the edge of the stone. He strained to see what lay at the far edge of the room, curious if there was a door or an exit. But he couldn't see past the rows and rows of stone soldiers fading into the distance.

"Sammy, do you realize that when we step off this stone, it's all gonna turn to rubbish?" Bart asked.

Sammy nodded. "What do you think they'll do?"

"Don't know. They sure ain't here for decoration."

"Yeah, but they're just... magic statues... right?" Sammy asked hopefully.

"You catch on quick, you do," Bart said.

Sammy caught a glimpse of something white flitter past a rank of archers. "Something's out there."

Bart continued to check his map. "Lots of things are out there, and they've got big stone swords to chop us with."

Sammy retreated back to the center of the circle. "No. I saw something move, something white."

Bart tucked his map and compass into his breast pocket. "What was it?"

Sammy peered through the circle for another look, but whatever had been there was gone. "I don't know."

Bart pointed to the wall far off to his left. "We've got to go that way. The map shows a door in the wall at the far end. We're in the middle. No use in wasting time running around in circles. Better head straight for it before things get too interesting."

Sammy cocked his brow. "So we just go?"

Bart crept to the edge of the stone and stretched his legs. "I suggest we run for it, straight to the door. These blokes are sure to wake up as soon as we step off the platform. Let's hope they're as slow as they are big."

Sammy lined up beside Bart and put his strong leg to the rear, like his school's track team did. He pointed. "Between those two groups and straight ahead?"

Bart inhaled deeply. "Right. Whenever you're ready."

Sammy inhaled three quick breaths. "Ready when you are."

"One, two, three." Bart darted through the huge stone knights that lined the circle. Sammy shot out after him.

They ran through the ranks of solders as fast as their legs would carry them. Sammy didn't see any movement at first. Then he caught a glimpse of white to his right, then to his left.

His lungs ached, and his legs ached. He and Bart were nowhere near the door. Pain seized Sammy's side. He couldn't continue on at that speed. "Go," he yelled. "I'll catch up."

Bart was already ten paces ahead. He slowed so Sammy could catch up. "No, you won't. Don't stop."

The pain in his side grew. He couldn't go on. He bent over, his hands on his knees, sucking in all the air the room would allow. Huge swords loomed over him.

The knights came to life, raising their swords high, ready to chop down.

Bart grabbed Sammy by the arm and pulled him away just in time before a huge broadsword crashed down and broke apart on the stone floor.

Bart pulled Sammy upright and pushed him forward. "Come on, you pudgy bugger. No stopping, I said."

All the statues had awoken and were converging on them, closing the gaps between the ranks. Sammy and Bart weren't even close to the far wall.

"We've got to split up," Bart said. "They can't catch us both. Meet you at the end. Take this in case you get cornered." Bart shoved a vial into Sammy's fist and was gone.

Sammy's path was blocked. The solders had cut off the path ahead. He doubled back. He was cut off again. He shot left, then right, then back again. Everywhere he ran, there they were. They moved slowly but were closing in. Given enough time, they would have him surrounded.

Stone crashed in the distance. Bart's words echoed through the hall. "Too slow, blockhead."

Sammy kept going, dodging left and right. By the skin of his teeth, he was able to avoid being bludgeoned by a giant marble axe. Spears crashed all around him. Rubble covered the stone floor. He slipped more than once but managed to keep away from the killer stone knights, but he was only slightly closer to the far wall.

A black granite arrow whizzed by Sammy's head and crashed into a stone knight who was about to crush him. The arrow broke into a million pieces, leaving behind a cloud of dust. Then another arrow smashed into the soldier's belly, and another. Sammy broke away and fled farther from the flying death bolts. He managed to get some space between himself and the hordes of knights and caught a glimpse of the archers that were shooting arrows. They turned their arrows on Bart. From that distance, Sammy could barely see him. He was probably at the door, because it looked as though he was staying in the same area rather than running all over the place like Sammy was.

He had to get back to Bart. If Bart had found the door, then Sammy was holding him up. Bart couldn't dodge arrows and swords forever while Sammy ran around in circles. Dozens of knights had already converged on Bart, and he wouldn't last long with those odds.

The white blur ran across Sammy's path again. This time, he got a better view. It was a white statue, not much taller than he was. It wore a braided silver chain around its neck. It had to be the Lead. If the morsels calmed the prisoners, then the Lead would calm the knights. Sammy didn't want Bart to be crushed, but he had no choice but to follow the white statue. It was too close to pass up. Sammy pursued.

The white statue was fast, but Sammy stayed behind it. He noticed it was faster in a straight line than on turns. It outpaced him, so he chased it toward a wall. It zipped along the perimeter of the room. *Great!* He hoped it stayed its course, right toward Bart. Maybe Bart could intercept it.

Finally, it reached a corner and followed the wall to the left. Sammy was on its tail. The turn slowed it down enough for him to catch up a little. He was out of breath, and his side ached, but he couldn't give up. Not this time. He was so close.

Bart came into view. He was surrounded by the mounted knights. Sammy didn't know how, but he had to gain on the white statue. He was close enough that he could see wings flapping on its feet and on its helmet.

The mounted knights drew closer to Bart. They had him surrounded. Each horse reared up on its hind legs and stomped down inches from Bart. He was able to dodge the giant, powerful stone horse legs, but that wouldn't last.

Sammy gained on the white statue a little more. He was right behind it. The silver chain trailed in the wind. Sammy was only a few feet away. His eyes darted back and forth between Bart and the white statue. Bart evaded a hoof but lost his footing. He slipped and fell onto his back. One of the horses reared up and was about to stomp down onto his chest. Sammy's eyes grew large.

In one last desperate surge to close the gap, Sammy pushed with all he had. He reached out for the Lead. He almost had it, but the white statue seemed to change gears and flew off at twice its previous speed. All hope was lost. Bart was going to be crushed, and it was Sammy's fault. If he had stuck close to Bart, they would have been through the door already.

The vial. What's in the vial?

Bart had given it to him for a reason. Sammy didn't know what it was, but he hoped drinking it couldn't hurt. If there was a time for last-ditch efforts, it was then. Sammy dug the vial from his pocket. The blue liquid bubbled when he uncorked it. He downed it in one gulp.

Sammy felt a powerful surge of energy run up his legs. He pushed off the ground and went flying through the air. He fell onto the white statue's head. It bucked, but Sammy held tightly with all the strength he could muster. His hands wrapped around the statue's neck and face, and his legs gripped under its shoulders. He grabbed the Lead and yanked on it. The braided silver chain cut through the soft stone, and the statue's head flew off, crashing against the hard floor. The body collapsed into a pile of rubble under him. He tumbled over the crumbled mess.

He had the Lead. It worked. The knights froze. The potion's power faded as Sammy sprinted over to his friend. Bart lay on his back, a stone hoof barely touching his chest.

Bart exhaled, his chest pushing up into the hoof. "You couldn't take any longer?"

Sammy took Bart's hand and pulled him out from under the horse. "Any closer, and your inside parts would be outside parts."

Bart pointed to Sammy's clenched fist that held the silver braided chain. "Where was it, the Lead?"

"On a white statue, the thing I saw before. Come. I'll show you." They walked back to the pile of rubble, and Sammy pointed to the remnants.

Bart cocked his head to the side. "Is that a winged helmet and sandals?"

Sammy picked up one of the helmet's broken wings. "Yeah. It was soft, like chalk."

Bart pointed at the wing in Sammy's hand. "Well, that takes the cake, don't it? Mercury's wings." Bart rubbed the crumbled stone between his fingers.

Sammy picked up the empty vial. "What's special about the wings? Really dope jumping potion, by the way. I couldn't have caught up to it on my own."

Bart chuckled. "Hope you ain't allergic to molted cricket skins. They're the main ingredient. Oh yeah, the wings. I keep forgetting, you're a normal, or at least, you were. They're a symbol of the god of passage to the next world."

Sammy raised his eyebrows. "You mean like angel wings?"

Bart dusted himself off. "No, older than all of that. Mercury, Hermes, Mearc, Mark, Cymro, helmets and wings, all names and symbols for the same guy. Come on. Let's go find that door."

Sammy followed Bart to the far wall. "The next world, like hell? Are you saying we're going to meet an angel of death who's gonna take us to hell? Because that's kind of serious."

Bart examined the stone wall. "No, bloke. It was just a statue, but the implication is that we're going somewhere down, somewhere dank, where things go to die. Help me find a knob or something." Bart pointed to a small indentation in the wall. "Look over here."

Sammy examined the Lead. Its intricate braiding and handle sparkled in the torchlight. He held the Lead up to the wall. A small metal wing protruded from the end of the handle. It matched up with the wing-shaped indentation Bart pointed out in the wall.

"Here goes nothing." Sammy pushed the Lead's handle into the wall. The wing-shaped protrusion slid into the wing-shaped indentation. It fit like a glove.

The cool breeze whispered in their ears again. "The Forever Knights are yours to command."

"You hear that? You're a commander twice over now. Come a long way, haven't we?" Bart smoothed his hand over the stone wall.

The stones ground, separating. A sarcophagus pushed its way out of the wall.

The dull black stone sarcophagus was cold to the touch and gave Sammy goose bumps. He rubbed his arms. "This thing is super creepy."

"A casket. How fitting." Bart pushed on the intricately carved cover. "Give us a hand."

Sammy helped Bart push the cover open. "These carvings show people coming out of the ground."

"In we go, then." Bart climbed into the coffin. "Roomy enough in here."

Sammy shook his head and climbed in after Bart. "It would be bigger on the inside, wouldn't it?" They lay on their backs, side by side, shoulders barely touching.

They slid the cover shut.

24

———

THE CRYPT KING

Sammy couldn't see. It was pitch black inside the sarcophagus. He tapped his finger on the inside of the cover. "Nothing's happening."

"I see that." Bart lit a match.

"What the heck are you doing? You're going to set us on fire or burn off all the oxygen. Where'd you get the matches anyway?" Sammy blew at the match, but it wouldn't go out.

"There's an inscription. I can't read it, though. It's older than I can tell. Ouch." The match burned Bart's fingers. "Where'd I get the matches, he says. Ain't you learned nothing yet? You just wait. Next, I'll pull a fuzzy rabbit from me topper."

Sammy pointed to a scene etched on the inside of the sarcophagus cover that looked like a graveyard. "The pictures, they're like the ones on the outside, people coming from the ground."

Bart pointed to a figure standing by a building. "Look at this one here. He's bigger than the rest."

"Get out," Sammy said. "We can flip it over and read it in the torchlight. Maybe there's a clue."

"Okay. One, two, three." Bart pushed the cover to the right, and Sammy helped. It fell over the side with a thud. They climbed out of the sarcophagus and found themselves in a different place.

Sammy's skin crawled. "This isn't the knight's room."

Bart looked at his map and compass. "But where are we?"

They were outdoors, in a graveyard. It was night, and the moon was full. Monuments and headstones littered the landscape. They weren't evenly spaced and lined up like Sammy thought they should be. They were haphazardly spaced, like the the glass bottles at a carnival ring toss.

"Look there." Bart pointed to a crypt far off in the distance. "That's where we're going. That's the next door."

Sammy was relieved to be outdoors again. The prison made him feel claustrophobic. "What are we doing outside? We've been in caves and tunnels and prisons until now." He breathed in the scent of freshly cut grass then smelled rotting flesh.

Bart looked about frantically. "Something's wrong."

Sammy looked behind him, expecting to see Frankenstein's monster or a mob of angry villagers. "Smells like roadkill."

"Whatever it is, it didn't die on a road," Bart said. "I'd wager it ain't even dead... completely."

Sammy tightened his laces and the steak's sling. If he had to run again, he would be prepared. "Completely, like not all the way? How can something be partially dead?"

Bart nodded to the crypt and stepped off. "We're going to find out, I'd wager. Let's go."

Sammy walked beside him. They heard moans and growls, hisses and snapping jaws. He flinched at a loud shriek in the distance. "You don't have another vial of jumping potion, do you? Or maybe a lightsaber?"

Bart pulled out the map and pointed out the moonlit monuments and the crypt in the distance. "Wish I did, but I'm fresh out."

They crept toward the crypt, anticipating the worst.

Sammy sneaked along as if he were a ninja from one of those '70s kung fu movies that reran every Saturday on the low-rent network. "Any idea of what's making those noises?"

They saw a figure in the distance, standing and waiting. It pointed at them. Sammy heard a scratchy, disembodied voice call out. "Brothers, sisters, awake."

Bart pointed to a hand emerging from the grass in front of a monument a few feet away. "Keep your wits about you. We've got company."

Sammy pointed to another hand pushing up from the earth on their other side. "They're coming up all over."

"Let's go." Bart tapped Sammy and trotted off.

Sammy jogged alongside Bart. "Why aren't we running faster?"

"They'll be a while. It's hard work crawling out of a grave. I should know. Besides, we need to save up our energies. After that tussle with the inmates and all that running about with the knights, I'm a bit worn out."

Sammy looked back. "Yeah, I'm kind of hungry. An energy bar wouldn't hurt, and the smell of this steak is driving me crazy. My mouth hasn't stopped watering since I picked it up."

Sammy spotted five or six torsos sticking out of the ground. They moaned and groaned, clawing at the earth, pulling themselves free.

When Bart and Sammy reached the crypt, they found it surrounded by a high, wrought-iron fence. The tomb was a single-story, square marble building with a single-gated door in the front.

Sammy looked back. A dozen silhouetted figures lumbered toward them. "Now what?"

"We go in." Bart tried the gate. It was locked.

Sammy grabbed hold of the bars and pulled himself up and over, just like he'd done so many times playing Man Hunt with the other kids from the group home. "No magical keys?"

Bart hoisted himself up and over the bars. "Not today."

Dozens of figures approached, trudging through the moonlight.

Sammy tried the gate on the door. It was locked. "There's more of them now."

Bart studied the lock. "I bet there are."

A deep groan bellowed from the back side of the crypt. Sammy ran around to investigate. Dozens of men, women, and children of all sizes were pressed up against the iron fence. Their eyes were hazy, and they smelled of rotting flesh.

Sammy ran back around to the front of the crypt. "They're here."

Bart stood in front of the barred door, muttering to himself with his eyes closed.

The crowd of about forty or fifty reached the crypt's front gate. They pushed on the fence from all sides. The crypt was surrounded.

Sammy smoothed his hands over each slab of the marble crypt. He poked and prodded every joint, anything that could be a lever. He'd seen too many old movies. "Come on, Magic Man. Think of something."

Dozens more came. They pushed up against the fence, and it swayed under their weight. They piled up and climbed over each other, reaching.

Sammy ran around the crypt again. Their numbers were increasing by the moment. "We need to do something, Bart. You've got to have a trick up your sleeve."

Bart adjusted the rune tied to his finger and slammed the door. "It's no use. I can't discern the nature of the door. It's like there's no way in."

The fence gave out. The reachers flooded in around the crypt.

Sammy clasped his hands together and gave Bart a boost up to the crypt's roof. "Nowhere to go but up."

Then, Bart hoisted Sammy up. Bart knelt down, feeling the marble, but there was nothing but smooth stone, no skylight and no entrance. "Nothing up here either. I was hoping there'd be a skylight or something."

The lumbering mob laid the fence down. Sammy couldn't even see it anymore. He only saw them, hundreds of them.

They pressed up against the side of the crypt, hands grabbing over the edges of the roof.

Bart chuckled. "Sammy, it's been very nice knowing you."

The grabbers clawed over one another, moaning. They piled on top of each other, groaning and crushing the ones at the bottom. Snapping and mutilating each other, they pulled their way up the side of the crypt.

"Knights, Edmond, help!" Sammy yelled. No help came.

"They won't come," Bart said. "A house divided against itself and all that."

It was over. There was no way out of this. Sammy searched for an escape, but there was nowhere to run.

Bart sat with his legs crossed and eyes closed, muttering to himself.

A load roar came from the graveyard. A giant man

shoved his way through the crowd of mindless reachers. The man tromped over the fallen fence and stood at the front of the crypt before Sammy even realized what was happening.

"Look!" Sammy shouted, pulling Bart out of his trance.

The first of the grabbers made it up onto the back side of the roof, then the next.

"I'm not going to sit here and do nothing," Sammy said. "We've got the runes. We have to fight like we did in the prison." He backed up, took a running start, and jumped off the roof into the crowd of reachers. He punched and knocked at the mindless groaners, and they flew in all directions, clearing a circle.

The roaring man smiled. "You have old magic, but you will fall." The giant raised his powerful fists over his head and brought them down onto Sammy.

Sammy raised his ringed hand over his head. The fists crashed into Sammy's arm with a flash of blue light. The blow had no power.

The roaring man screamed and clenched his wrist in agony. The ring had acted as a shield and redirected the energy back at him. "Your tricks won't last forever." The man reared up again, raised his arms high and screamed a war cry that sounded like coming doom.

Sammy raised his arm again, but the rune flew from his finger. Without the ring to block the blow, he would be crushed.

The huge arms flew down at Sammy. He braced, squeezed his eyes shut, and hoped for a quick end, but it didn't come.

Sammy opened his eyes and saw the man still and motionless, a green glow around him.

Green light flowed from Bart's hands into the big man's

chest. Bart was dripping wet with sweat, agony written clearly across his face. "Grab it, the harness," Bart stuttered.

The big man wore two black leather straps across his chest. They were attached to a silver circle of metal. Sammy grabbed the metal ring and pulled with all his might. The green light flowed through the metal ring into his arm. He lost control of his body, trembling. He fell back, still clutching the ring. Then everything faded to black.

Sammy awoke lying on fresh grass. Bart sat beside him, his head hung low, breathing heavily. Sammy's body ached as if he'd been beaten with a thousand clubs. "Ow. What happened?"

The mindless reachers meandered about in no particular direction.

Bart nodded to the leather straps in Sammy's open hand. "You got it, the harness."

"The green light?" Sammy asked.

"I had to stop him. Here's your rune. I found it in the grass." Bart tossed the rune, and his arm fell limply to his side.

"Where is he?" Sammy asked.

"He's over there by the door."

The giant bald man stood at the crypt door, watching and waiting.

Bart looked different. His frowning face was lined, and he had a patch of white hair in the front where it had been black before.

"You don't look so good," Sammy said.

"I used all my energy to stop him from pounding you," Bart said. "Probably took ten years off my life. You're welcome, by the way."

Sammy stood. "Thank you. We've got to find you some food."

"I'll be all right. I just need to sit here a spell. Go on."

Sammy left Bart to rest. He went to the crypt's door and the big man. The tall bald giant's filthy chest was bare. He wore muddy torn trousers, but no shoes. His feet were black and rotted, covered in maggots. He smelled of death. The large man bowed and knelt on one knee. "Long live the King."

"King?" Sammy asked.

"The King of the Dead!" the giant man shouted. Most of the reachers were gone, but the ones that remained responded with groans and rumblings.

Sammy held his breath as long as he could. When he finally inhaled, he gagged but managed to keep his stomach in check. "I'm the King the of the Dead?" he asked. The title held no appeal.

"Your Highness, we must rest. If you please, I'll take my leave." The man's scratchy voice grated in Sammy's ears.

"Yeah, go rest."

"Call, and we'll come. By your leave, sir?"

Sammy nodded.

The giant pulled the heavy iron door open and plodded away.

"You wouldn't be stepping out on me, would you, Your Highness?" Bart seemed refreshed, like his old self.

"What'd you do, have a magic Red Bull or something?" Sammy asked.

"Much worse than all that, take my word for it."

"A minute ago, you looked like you were about to pass out." Sammy furrowed his brows. "Now you're fine."

"I merely made a slight speculation," Bart said. "It worked out in my favor."

Sammy blinked.

"Dark stuff I picked up from the Master, really too much

trouble to bother with, but this one time couldn't hurt, I hope," Bart said.

"You've got to teach me that one someday," Sammy said. "But we should see what's in here."

Bart went inside the crypt. "Come on then, Majesty."

25

THE WAY OUT

Sammy walked around the inside of the crypt. It smelled old, like mold and dust. He looked for anything that might be helpful, like magical mushrooms. But the room was empty except for a single wooden door squarely in the middle of the crypt. He pulled up on its ring, exposing marble stairs leading into the darkness below.

The cool breeze whispered in their ears. "The Army of Living Death is at your command."

"Wait, something's off," Bart said.

"What's wrong?" Sammy asked.

A booming voice bellowed in their ears. "The allotted time has passed. The seekers have become the keepers. A warning to followers: be gone and be free."

Panic rose up in Sammy's chest. "What's that mean?" But he already knew the answer. He'd been dreading this moment. If only he'd moved faster, done more.

Bart pursed his lips and put a consoling hand on Sammy's shoulder. "I'm sorry."

Sammy shook his head. "No."

"We tried. You know we did," Bart said.

"Stop talking like that. Come on. We have to save Elizabeth."

Bart pointed to the darkness beyond the door. "It's no use, mate. She's been here too long. The prison won't let her go now."

He refused to give up on Elizabeth, not after all he'd been through. They couldn't just steal someone's dog and get away with it. That wasn't how things were supposed to work. He shot Bart a cold sidelong glance and stepped down into the darkness. Bart followed.

They materialized in another cave. A blinding light shone from a passageway on their right. He saw the park's green grassy hills through the door. Elizabeth lay there in the green grass, waiting. Darkness poured from the passage on their left.

Sammy approached the dark passageway. "Let's go." Something crunched under his feet as if he was walking on potato chips. The crunching grew louder as he walked.

Bart pointed to the lighted passage. "No, mate. This way's out."

"I'm not leaving. You're not going to change my mind."

"Seekers, enter the light and never return. Enter the dark, never escape," a deep hollow voice said.

"Do you see? This here is it," Bart said. "There's no going back. It's giving you a way out. It's even giving you a new dog. Listen to reason."

"I'm getting out, but after I get Elizabeth, the real Elizabeth."

Bart's tone softened. "You ain't listening, chum. She's gone. It's got her, and it ain't letting her go."

"No. You're not listening," Sammy said. "I'm not leaving without her."

Bart shook his head and looked down. "Then you ain't leaving, friend. That's the long and the short of it."

Sammy slapped his ankle. The ground was covered with tiny beetles that were crawling up onto his legs. He kicked and shook them off, but it was no use. There was no getting away from them.

"You see the the beetles, don't you?" Bart asked. "The prison don't want us here. It's giving us the bum's rush, pushing us out."

"Or you don't want me here. Do you expect me to believe that if I abandon Elizabeth and walk through the light, you're coming with me? You're going to leave your master?"

Bart looked down. "Sure, you're right. He was my master for a time, but he ain't no more. He got locked up in here for them deeds he done, and they let me go, just like that. No penalty, no penance, nothing. They was all 'Thank you for your time. Now be on your way.' So what am I to do? No friends, no family. Only guilt eating me alive, day in, day out. So that's what I did. I find this here prison, and I learned its secrets. I made it safe from intruders, them who'd try to free Durga. You think if I wasn't here, them cultists wouldn't't've found him long ago? All these years I put in here, keeping them cultists out, keeping the prison safe, when I could've been out there in the light... that don't show for nothing?"

Sammy snorted. "That's right. Responsibility. It's my responsibility to get Elizabeth, and that's what I'm doing."

"Brother, you ain't got a snowball's chance in Antille. She's gone. I seen a dozen fellows get caught up in this madhouse. Sure, a few found their way back after the timer gone off, but they was gone, their minds turned to mush."

Sammy jabbed an accusing finger at Bart. "That won't happen to her. You know she's special. Are you coming or not?" The beetles were up to his knees. He waded through them as if he was in the ball pit at the Kid Zone Play Center. They were in his socks, biting at him. It felt like a million pinpricks.

Bart pointed to the dark passage. "You know I've got to stop Culty." He made a fist, pounding his thumb into his chest. "It's my responsibility, not yours."

"Well, let's go. If she's gone, then at least I tried. We've got to stop the cop anyway." The beetles reached up to Sammy's hips. "And at least I'll know I didn't abandon a friend in a time of need."

Bart exhaled. "I don't know what we'll find through that blackness. Probably Culty or maybe Durga himself. You willing to die, or worse? If we fail, we could end up with the prisoners in the hall, or in the graveyard, or tortured."

Sammy stepped into the darkness.

26

A CHILLING GRIP

Sammy stepped into another round cavern. Torches lined the walls. In the middle was a stone altar, like the one at the prison's entrance. Elizabeth Bennet lay on the altar, unconscious. A pale, scowling man with dark eyes was dressed in bloodred robes, standing over her. His hands were outstretched, and a blue mist flowed up from her body into his. The gold feoh rune hung around his neck on a gold necklace. Culty looked over the man's shoulder, grinning from ear to ear.

"Stop!" Sammy yelled. "Get away from her."

A white mist poured down and shrouded Elizabeth and the man in red robes. Sammy ran to them, but they were gone.

Culty slammed his hand down on the altar and pointed a filthy finger at Sammy. "He's the greatest wizard the world has ever known, and you think you can stop him, The Bringer of Order, of law, the One who'll bring back the old ways?"

Bart scowled. "You're delusional."

Sammy stomped toward the altar. "Where is she?" He felt his rune's power pulsing through his body.

Culty came around the altar to meet Sammy. "I've been waiting to teach you a lesson."

They met in front of the altar. Culty moved to take hold of Sammy's arm, but Sammy batted his hand away. He grabbed at Sammy with his other hand, but again, Sammy batted it away. Culty howled in rage. He reached for Sammy's throat. Sammy knocked the man's arms up over his head.

Sammy stepped back on his right leg. Power welled up inside him. "You enjoy picking on kids and little puppies? Well, I've got the power now, and you should know when you've been beat." He shot his arm out, pushing his palm straight into the man's huge belly.

The blow knocked Culty back into the altar. He regained his footing and charged Sammy as if he were a bull. "Argh." Culty grunted, catching Sammy in a bear hug, wrapping his big hairy arms around Sammy like a vise. Sammy gasped for air, but it was no use. His lungs were being crushed, his consciousness fading by the second.

Through half-open eyes, Sammy saw Bart box the man's ears. The man howled and flung Sammy aside. Sammy lay on the stone floor, blinking.

Culty charged Bart, but Bart stuck his foot out and stepped aside. "Not this time, bozo."

Culty tripped over Bart's outstretched leg and tumbled to the ground.

Sammy caught his breath and found his footing. He focused on his rune and its power. Energy pulsed through his arm with each labored breath.

Bart closed his eyes, holding his hands up in front of him. Culty charged Bart again.

"What are you doing?" Sammy shouted. "He'll kill you. Defend yourself." Sammy jumped in between them. If Culty got a hold of Bart, it would all be over.

He was too slow. Culty and Bart locked fingers like school kids on the playground. Sammy's jaw dropped open when Bart's hands glowed with an eerie blue light. They smoked like ice cubes in an open freezer.

In the span of a second, Culty's expression changed from hatred to shock and fear.

Bart grinned. "Got a bit of a chill, do we?"

Culty dropped to his knees. "Argh."

Instinctually, Sammy wrapped his hands around Culty's head. He concentrated on the rune and its power. A bolt of energy shot though Sammy's fingers into the man's temples. His body jerked and slumped. Bart released him, and he fell into a crumpled heap.

Sammy grabbed the cop by the arm, finding it cold to the touch. He squeezed. "Where is she?"

Culty winced and squirmed. "You're breaking my arm."

Bart seethed. "Looks like the shoe's on the other foot, ain't it?"

Sammy squeezed harder. "Doesn't feel good, does it? Either you tell me where Elizabeth is right now, or it's going to get a lot worse."

The man cried out.

Bart put a hand on Sammy's wrist. "We ain't like him, brother."

Sammy released Culty's arm. The cop pulled a glass vial from his pocket and gave it to Sammy. "Here."

Sammy took the vial. "What's this?"

Bart pulled two long black shoelaces from his breast pocket and bound the man's ankles. "How'd an ignorant brute like you get your filthy hands on a mist vial?"

"We found them, searching for him," Culty said. "Got one from an exhibit at the Natural History Museum, dug one up in the graveyard on Twenty-Second, got a few more. I think he left them just in case."

"Sounds about right," Bart spat. "He'd leave a few lying around in case he needed to make a quick getaway."

"Where's Elizabeth?" Sammy asked again.

"Break the vial," Bart said. "Walk into the mist. They'll be there."

Sammy removed the handcuffs from the brute's belt and locked them around the man's sweaty wrists.

Bart reached into his breast pocket and pulled out a small, shriveled red berry. "It's not enough. Here, eat this, scummer." He shoved the shriveled berry into the cop's mouth. The man fell asleep and snored like a walrus.

"He'll be out for at least a day," Bart said.

Sammy threw the mist vial at the stone floor. A white cloud puffed up, enveloping them, transporting them to somewhere else.

27

TEAMWORK TAKEDOWN

Bright flashes of red light reflected through the dissipating mist, like the lasers and fog machine at the roller rink.

Bart grabbed Sammy by the shoulders and yanked him to safety. They crouched behind an altar like the one at the start of the maze. Twelve altars in the round room circled an open space in the middle. Lord Durga was in the middle, and Elizabeth's limp body was tucked under his arm.

Durga shot bolts of red light from his open hand. They crashed into the stone wall behind Bart and Sammy. Chunks of stone fell from the wall.

Sammy pushed Bart away. "I'm not hiding."

Bart pulled Sammy back again. "You see the red death bullets breaking the stone, don't you? Think of what they'll do to your head."

Elizabeth whimpered. The sound echoed in Sammy's ears. She was so close. Sammy couldn't allow the man to hurt her anymore. He had to get to her. He ran out into the line of fire, heading straight for Durga. Elizabeth disappeared from Durga's arms.

Durga cackled. "Brave boy. Yes, come to Master. I have your reward."

Sammy was still twenty feet away, but closing quickly. "I'm coming, and I've got something for you."

Durga unleashed a flurry of red energy bolts from his hands. "More foolish than brave, I see."

The bolts broke apart on Sammy's chest. Sammy's ring burned hot on his finger. "You're going down." He was almost there, only a few feet away, but then he was caught around the throat by some invisible hand. It gripped his neck and pulled him off his feet, holding him in the air, eye level with the evil Lord Durga. Sammy couldn't breathe. He grabbed at his neck, but there was nothing to take hold of.

Durga cackled. "Yes, foolish, foolish boy. I had previously imagined we could be friends. I am recently in need of a good apprentice. Isn't that right, Bartholomew?"

Bart shot out from behind the altar and threw a sharp stone at Durga. Durga waved a hand, and the stone halted in midair and fell to the ground. He laughed and looked upward. "This is your champion, a stone thrower?" he yelled.

Bart smiled. He drew a clear, sparkling oblong crystal from his breast pocket and hurled it at Durga. It broke apart on Durga's face, and steam rose from the shattered pieces. "Pride goeth before destruction, don't it, Durga?"

Durga screamed and held his face. The pungent odor of rotted eggs filled the space. Sammy fell to the ground and caught his breath. He closed the remaining few feet between him and Durga and thrust his ring into the tall man's stomach. Durga clutched his stomach and hunched over. The rune still had power.

"The knights," Bart yelled.

Sammy remembered Edmond's offer of help. "Edmond, help! Knights, Dead, help!"

Lord Durga stood upright and threw more red death bolts at Sammy. Sammy held up his ring, and the bolts bounced off of it. But with each hit, he slid farther back, the force pushing harder and harder. Sammy's energy drained more and more with each blow. He couldn't deflect the barrage much longer.

Bart pushed Sammy aside, taking the force of the blows. The bolts bounced off Bart's ring, but the energy drain was evident. Bart winced with each blow.

Edmond burst out from behind one of the altars. He bounded at Durga and crashed down onto the man's head. Bart pulled Sammy by the arm, retreating behind an altar.

Durga's hand grew into a ball of bloodred light, popping and buzzing with energy. He thrust it into Edmond's chest. The giant flew into the wall and collapsed onto the floor. "Your soldiers won't protect—"

A stone knight on horseback emerged from behind an altar. It charged at Durga. The horse reared up, and the knight slammed a granite sword down onto Durga's shoulder.

The former King of the Dead popped up from behind an altar and leapt at Durga. He clamped onto Durga's arm, biting down with his vise-like jaws.

Stone knights and dead reachers emerged from behind the twelve altars, filing out into the room.

Sammy and Bart crouched behind the altar, catching their breath. "Use the Lead," Bart said.

The Knights, Dead, and Prisoners filled the room, cutting off access to Lord Durga. They surrounded him. A red globe grew around the evil man and exploded in a shower of blinding light. The Knights, Dead, and Prisoners flew through the air and slammed into the walls. They lay there twitching. More Knights, Dead, and Prisoners appeared from behind the altars. Lord Durga shot them down with his red bolts, one by one.

"He's distracted," Bart whispered.

Sammy clutched the Lead and handed the Harness to Bart. "Together."

Durga pivoted on his heels, shooting bolts of red fury from his fingertips. The bolts shattered upon the knights. Bits of stone whizzed every which way. The Prisoners and the Dead fell one by one, the red bolts breaking apart on their chests, sending them flying into a mass of crumpled bodies.

Together, Sammy and Bart snuck up behind the distracted Durga. Sammy jumped up onto Durga's back and wrapped the Lead around his neck. It slithered like a snake and wove itself into a flat silver collar. A braided silver cord grew from it and crawled back into Sammy's grip. Bart reached around and shoved the harness's silver circlet into Durga's chest. The leather straps flew around Durga's arms, binding them to his torso then snapping back onto the circle. Durga struggled. There was a flash of red light, and everything disappeared.

28

A MARIONETTE PARTY

Sammy blinked. When he opened his eyes, he found himself alone in an empty open space. There was no floor or ceiling, nothing to see at all, only a field of white in every direction.

He stomped his foot down, but no sound came from it. He had to be standing on something because he wasn't floating, but then again, there was no floor.

Sammy guffawed. "Stupid magic."

Footsteps echoed behind him. Sammy spun around. Durga was there, only five feet away. He wore a slick gray suit and shiny black shoes. He smiled and held his arms open as if he were greeting an old friend. Sammy was confused. Durga took Sammy's hand and shook it warmly. "My boy, you've done well for yourself. Very impressive, I must admit. What shall it be then, hmm?"

Sammy recoiled. "What are you talking about? Where's Elizabeth? Where's Bart? What is this place?" Sammy stepped back, unsure what had happened.

Durga backed up and showed his palms. "I mean you no harm, my boy. Don't you understand? You've won our little competition. And to the victor go the spoils, do they not? What is it you desire?"

Sammy barked, "Get me out of here and take me to Elizabeth. You can't have her."

Durga chuckled. "Yes, the dog. It all started with your little friend, didn't it? And there she is." Durga waved his arm.

Sammy realized he was standing on a little hill, overlooking a cottage on a pond. Elizabeth played near the water's edge. She batted her paw at the still water.

"You see, happy and healthy," Durga said. "That is what you wanted, to have her back? Go to her."

Sammy inhaled the fresh spring air. He took a step toward the pond. "But we were in the prison."

Durga spoke softly. "Prisons and ponds, what's the difference really? What matters is there's your little dog, and look. She has a friend."

A gray Great Dane barked at a red koi fish in the pond. Elizabeth jumped up onto the Dane's back. It ran in circles while Elizabeth rode it. She seemed to enjoy it immensely.

Sammy pointed. "I know that other dog. I saw it before." He took another step down the slight hill.

"And look, your friends are here too," Durga said. A tall girl walked out of the cabin. The two dogs ran to her. They rolled in the green grass. The Dane nudged her hand with its nose while Elizabeth nibbled at her long, dark hair.

Sammy enjoyed the smell of fresh cut grass and oranges. He stepped closer to the cottage. "Yeah, my friends."

Bart was there too. Colorful bubbles flowed from his fingertips. Elizabeth jumped up, popping them with her nose. Sammy stepped down to the bottom of the hill.

"You recall when Bart fell in the water, don't you?" Durga asked.

A canoe tied to a little dock bobbed up and down on the still water.

Sammy nodded, smiling. "Oh yeah. I do remember. I told him not to stand up in the canoe. He didn't listen. It was so funny. We laughed until our sides hurt."

Durga led Sammy around to the front of the cottage. Bart sat at a picnic table covered in a red-and-white tablecloth. Sammy sat down next to him. "Good thing it's time for a luncheon. I'm famished."

Bart passed the mashed potatoes. "Your mum's the best cook in the whole wide world. Her meatloaf is to die for."

Sammy took the potatoes. He spooned a heaping portion onto his plate. He stared at the plate. It reminded him of something, but he couldn't remember what.

"Who's ready for dessert?" Sammy's mother asked. She placed a warm golden-brown pie on the table. She smiled, her teeth sparkling in her wide mouth. She handed Sammy a plate. It smelled like sweet cinnamon. He took the plate and stared at it.

Sammy's mother sat. Her classic white dress sparkled in the sunshine. "You know, your father and I got you a little gift because you're doing so well in school."

Sammy couldn't take his eyes off of the pie plate. Something was off about it.

"Yes, you've been doing quite well," Durga said. "Your mother and I got you one of those... what was it that you asked for when we tossed rings at the fair?"

Sammy nodded. "A video game, the one with the virtual reality." *Virtual reality.* "It's a game that feels like real life, but it's not." He remembered the white plate in the tunnel at the park. He thought of the pale hand that had grabbed Elizabeth and pulled her through the bars.

Sammy shot up from the table and threw the pie plate at

Durga. "You're not my father." He glared at the woman. "She's not my mother." He pointed to the dog lying in the grass. "And that's not Elizabeth."

Durga scowled. His gray suit was gone, and he was back in his red robe. The woman's smiling face cracked as if it was made of glass. But it wasn't made of glass. It was porcelain. They were all porcelain and cloth, life-size puppets with strings attached to their hands. The puppets fell limp. The fake Elizabeth keeled over and lay there, lifeless.

The sky cracked as though a bolt of lightning had shot through it. The scene crumbled around Sammy, and in an instant, he was back with the real Bart and Durga, still bound by shackles.

29

A BROKEN CONTRACT

The red light dissipated. Bart was back in the study from so long ago. He peered out the window. The gardener tended a hedgerow.

"You've done it, my boy, completed your training." Durga slapped Bart on the shoulder like he would an old friend. "But you're no boy anymore. You've grown into a man, and a fine one at that. Why, you've honed your skills to a point. I couldn't be prouder."

Bart poured a glass of sherry. "I did me best. Wasn't easy on me own."

"I dare say you worked it out splendidly." Durga motioned to the chair behind the desk. "Take your place. You've earned it."

Bart sat behind the desk. The soft cushion cradled him like a mother's love. "Is it mine now?"

Durga sat opposite Bart. "All of it. I've got plans to the East, so you'll head up operations here."

Bart straightened the desk blotter and inkwell. "I'll make a go of it."

Durga pulled an envelope from the breast pocket of his

fine gray jacket. "I should say you shall." He laid the envelope on the desk.

Bart picked it up. "Head of operations, you say? Now what all does that entail?"

Durga looked at the envelope. "We're equals now. Do as you see fit. I trust that you should manage properly."

Bart pulled a contract from the envelope. "'Equals, you say?" The word echoed in his mind.

Durga laid a red quill next to the inkwell. "Just make your mark there. It's all good and proper. You've my word on that account."

Bart skimmed the contract. "I always was rubbish with me letters."

Durga tapped the desk impatiently. "Make your mark, Bartholomew. We haven't time."

Bart looked at the contract. "Equals?" His eyes found a spot on the floor across the room, the spot where he had first learned of Durga's horrid lust for power and his capacity to exact pain. Bart squinted as if he was seeing Durga for the first time. "You're gonna share power with me?" He snickered.

Durga slammed his hand down on the desk, and the sleeve of his red robes shone stark against the dark wood. "Make your mark, Bart."

Bart sneered. "Is this all you've got left? Little mind games in the dark?" He laughed. "Have you forgotten? Do you not remember how many men I sent here for you? All them prisoners back there? I put them here for you. And now you want to trap me here with 'em? I stayed here in your little prison for so long with all its temptations. You can't fool me anymore. The council done right in keeping you here, and here you'll stay, much longer."

Bart tore the contract in half, and in a flash, he was back with Sammy. Durga was bound with the harness.

30

THE PRINCESS WAKES

Sammy shook the cobwebs from his head, and with a trembling hand, shoved a bit of steak into Lord Durga's mouth. "I almost lost it, just like at the arches. Did he confuse you too?"

Bart exhaled, his chest heaving. Sweat dripped from his brow. "Yeah. Had me going for a minute there, but I saw through his tricks."

They each contemplated their hallucinations for a long, silent moment.

Sammy held up the steak. "This'll put a stop to his tricks, make him tell us where Elizabeth is."

Durga wobbled, a dazed look about him.

"Looks like the steak worked." Sammy examined his ring finger. It burned. The rune was red hot. It melted into Sammy's skin. "Bart, what's happening?"

"I know," Bart said. "Me too."

The rune disappeared. It completely melted away, leaving a blister in its place. Sammy's finger ached. A pain grew up into his hand and wrist. "What's going on?"

Bart massaged his wrist. "Don't know."

Sammy looked at Durga and pointed to the floor. The man dropped to his knees. Sammy pointed to the rune hanging around Durga's neck. "Is it like ours?"

"Ancient charm symbols," Bart said. "I'd be surprised if it weren't."

"Give it to me," Sammy said to Durga.

Lord Durga removed the gold necklace and handed it to Sammy.

"What happened to our runes?" Sammy asked. "Why did they burn away?"

Lord Durga responded in a dull drone. "They have not gone away. They have been absorbed into your auras. I cannot know for sure without proper experimentation, but I hypothesize that the energy bolts overheated the metal, which required the runes to cool themselves. The body, unable to provide relief, offered the runes to the aura, which in turn absorbed the energy, thus causing the rune and its powers to be infused into the aura."

Bart raised his eyebrows. "Are you saying I've got rune powers?"

Durga blinked and nodded.

Sammy thought it seemed a bit far-fetched, but what hadn't been strange about that day? He had more important things to think about. "Call your servant, the cop. We're taking him to a real jail."

The cultist appeared unconscious on the floor.

"It'd be better to leave him here in the prison," Bart said.

"I've got an idea," Sammy said. "Bring Elizabeth here now."

His eyes closed. The motionless puppy appeared on the floor beside the cop. Her rune was still attached to her harness.

Sammy knelt down and stroked her hair. "What's wrong with her?"

"She resisted sharing her aura," Durga droned. "She fought..."

A lump grew in Sammy's throat. "If you hurt her—"

Elizabeth snorted in her sleep.

Bart tapped Sammy's arm. "Hold on, brother. She's all right."

"The dog is merely asleep," Durga said. "She'll awaken with the sunlight."

Sammy exhaled. He picked the puppy up and held her in his arms. He stroked her head and inhaled her oatmeal shampoo.

"Your magic, I want you to give it to Bart," Sammy said. "You're a horrible puppy-napper. He'll do good with it."

Bart shook his head. "I don't want his filth. Don't know what it'll do to me. Could corrupt my good nature and turn me into the likes of him."

Durga held out a hand. A cracked and frayed leather-bound tome materialized in his open palm.

"You'll know what to do," Sammy said. "You'll use it for good." He took the book and handed it to Bart. "We're going to make it so they never do anything like this again." He pointed to the dirty cop. "Remove his memory, but make him remember one thing, that he and Lord Durga challenged Bartholomew Baker and lost."

Durga's sleepy eyes blinked, and he nodded. "I have done so."

"We'll send him back where he came from as a warning," Sammy said.

Bart agreed. "I like it."

The broken pieces of stone soldiers on the ground moved. They gathered together and reformed into horses and knights. They went back through the altars, one by one. The Army of the Dead followed. Edmond, the King of the Dead, and the winged statue stood by.

"Listen, everyone," Sammy said. "We're gonna make some changes and beef up security because the old way didn't work. Edmond is the new commander of all the armies. I want Durga under guard at all times, and I want patrols throughout every part of the prison. Lock it down. No one gets in or out."

"Yes, sir," Edmond said.

"Guards control the Lead at all times," Sammy said. "The Lead and harness stay on Durga always, forever."

Edmond bowed. "Yes, sir."

Sammy turned to Durga. "If anyone gets through, you turn them away. You don't want their help, understand?"

"I don't want help," Lord Durga said.

"That's it, then," Bart said. "Let's see if we can't get you and your pup on your way."

"No, not just us. You're coming too."

Bart looked at the ground and shrugged. "I've been here a long time. There's nothing for me out there in the world."

"Too long," Sammy said. "It's time you forgive yourself and live your life."

Bart sighed. "You're right. I may have been here too long, forgot what life's all about. Besides, I can keep a watch from the outside, make sure them cultists keep out of my park. But how do we get out?"

The prison whispered in their ears. "The ways are parted. Peace to you."

An opening appeared in the stone wall, leading to the park outside. The sun's rays shone through.

Sammy stroked Elizabeth's fur. "You ready, Bart?"

Bart dragged Culty's heavy, limp body to the opening and shoved it through. "I hope so."

They stepped through the opening into the sunshine. Elizabeth woke up and licked Sammy's cheek.

31

AN OFFER OF EMPLOYMENT

Days later, Bartholomew Baker stood alone before the Council of Protection, among the stars, in the Halls of Knowing.

Erland Skuld shook Bart's hand with a smile. "Bartholomew Baker, what have you to say for yourself?"

Bart dropped the Durga's tome. Though there wasn't any floor at all, it landed without a bang. "I don't want it."

"But sadly, it is yours. The universal rules of craft work and proper form dictate as much," Skuld said.

Bart shot Skuld a steely glance. "I ain't interested in rules or his magic."

Skuld raised his eyebrows. "Regrettably, you cannot give this book away, but I may have an idea that could remedy your particular predicament." Skuld made eye contact with several council members seated throughout the room.

The council erupted. They waved their hands and slammed the tables. Bart couldn't hear a word. It may have been a simple deafening spell but was probably much more powerful craftwork. Bart couldn't tell. His senses were turned upside down.

"You've shown great promise," Skuld said once it had quieted down. "We've decided to help you with your book problem. We'll house it for you, but you can have it back whenever you like."

Bart shook his head. "I don't want it back. Do with it what you like. Throw it off a cliff or bury it under the ocean for all I care."

"But there it is," Skuld said. "Should you choose to claim your property, it will be here. You may enter and take possession if you feel the need. Very few mortals have been made privy of this council, and none given access as they like. It is unprecedented, but your circumstance warrants it so."

"Don't trouble yourself. I won't be back. I've got things to do, a life to live."

"You have a great talent for the art," Skuld said. "Should you be so inclined as to inquire of an apprenticeship position..."

Bart shook his head. "I don't want that. Had an apprenticeship once. Didn't work out. Go it on my own this time."

"Nevertheless, I suggest you seek out the one some call the Wizard of Time. He may be of service, should you so desire," Skuld said. "And the prison, it is gone. It needs your protection no longer."

"It's gone?" Bart asked. "Where'd it go? Who's gonna make sure them cultists don't give it another go, then?"

"We've moved it to the Desert of Forgetting," Skuld said. "It's safer there. We could have avoided this whole mess if we'd placed it there at the start, but that time has passed. The point is you are free. You are under no obligation to keep it safe. Your crimes have been paid for, many times over, child. Do not seek it out. Only pain lies within. Be free and enjoy your life. You deserve it."

32

THE LIBRARY OF TIME

Bart sat at one of the library's reading tables with several gray-haired men. He looked up at them and steepled his fingers. "All right then, Mr. Thomas. I'll tell you what. You teach me your world-renowned trans-configuration method, and I'll share with you old Mrs. Bailey's chicken soup recipe as well as my method of ulti-mate seeing. I'd like to soar as an eagle, and I assume you'd enjoy peeping in on a shareholders' meeting or two."

The group grumbled. Bart had never offered his ulti-mate seeing method. The stakes were as high as they would get.

Mr. Thomas peeked through the high stacks of dusty books on the table. His overgrown white eyebrows obscured his bright-blue eyes. "Mr. Bartholomew, you continue to astound. We sit here amongst the Lost Tomes of Time. Why, you are the youngest practitioner to have ever located the library. You can stay and study for as long as you like. You will neither hunger nor thirst, nor have a need for rest or sleep. All the world's magic is at your fingertips, and you continue to barter. I can show you what you desire, but wouldn't you benefit so much had you researched the spell for yourself? There is something to be said for a self-made man." He coughed.

Bart slapped his hand down on the table. "Very well then, Mr. Thomas, if you'd rather I speak with Mr. Santana, I hear his transmutation method is also highly regarded. I'm sure he'd be interested in hearing about my seeing method."

Mr. Thomas cleared his throat. "Mr. Bartholomew, please don't misunderstand my meaning. I meant no insult."

Mr. Santana leaned back in the plush armchair, puffing on his fine hand-rolled cigar. He sipped his sweet, aromatic cognac. "Mr. Baker, I've been paying close attention, and I must commend you on your actions. In the short time you've been studying here, you've managed to amass the largest collection of personal knowledge I've ever seen."

Bart snorted. "I'm a quick study."

Mr. Thomas snorted in kind. "And a fast talker."

Bart furrowed his brow and pointed a finger. "I've been straight with you, all of you. And if you don't want to share your method with me, Mr. Santana, I can do without. That goes double for you, Mr. Thomas."

The group grumbled.

Mr. Santana snapped his fingers, summoning a decanter of cognac. It appeared. His cufflinks clinked against the glass. "Come, Mr. Baker, don't be upset. I don't aim to injure, only inquire of your intentions. We all know of your past and that of your former mentor."

Bart shot Mr. Santana a steely, cold look. "You know about me, do you? You lazy lot sit up here in your ivory tower with your books for years on end, decades, millennia. He was down there on Earth, wreaking havoc, and you lot did nothing. Mr. Thomas, do we have a deal or not?"

Mr. Thomas handed Bart a scroll. "Yes, Mr. Baker. Here is

the method. Your offer for chicken soup was too tempting to pass on."

Bart took the scroll and placed it into his breast pocket. He took Mr. Thomas's soft, trembling hands in his own and held them. He looked past the white bushy eyebrows, deep into the man's blue eyes. Their hands glowed a green light. He tasted carrots, celery, and dill. The aroma of chicken soup wafted through the room. The light faded.

Bart stood, and the barest trace of a smile played across his mouth. "And there is your recipe for chicken soup as well as the method of seeing. It's been good doing business with you."

Mr. Santana sniffed the air and licked his lips. "So Mr. Baker, now you have it. Every spell, incantation, every method. The library's existed here for time immemorial, and wizards have studied here just as long. What will you do now that you no longer have a need for it?"

Bart jumped up, and the chair tumbled behind him. "And time out of mind, they been down there, scrambling, fighting for a bite to eat. Half the world ain't got enough food, and you up here snap your fingers for a continental breakfast and a glass of merlot!" Bart checked his temper. He straightened his suit then spun a globe on a pedestal. "As I was saying, the world's gone to the dogs, and you lot sit in here with your books and let it all happen. I mean to put a stop to it, the hardship, the pain, the starving children."

"You're just one man, you can't save the world, Bart," Mr. Thomas said hesitantly.

Bart pushed the globe, and it toppled to the floor and rolled under the table. The crash echoed through the halls. "I can, and I will, or I'll die trying. I'm going to find the Wizard of Time. He'll help."

Mr. Thomas retrieved the globe from under the table.

With a snap of his fingers, it popped back onto its pedestal. "Ah, the Savior of the Forgotten, of the Lost and the Damned."

A greedy smile flashed across Bart's wide mouth. "But first, I'm off to the market. I'll need supplies. I heard many a story of the wondrous trinkets sold there."

Mr. Santana threw up his hands. "Another young soul lost to the Market. Bart, you know great men have wasted their natural lives chasing after it. You'll never find it. Don't waste your best years, please."

"While you geezers had your nose stuck in them dusty tomes, I was doing a little research of my own, and I've found it. I've been following it for weeks, and I got the pattern, so I'll always know where to find it. And I ain't unlearning that little bit of useful information either."

Mr. Thomas clapped his hands together. "Ha ha, you are full of tricks, Mr. Baker. That you are."

Bart waved a hand, and two glasses of sparkling wine materialized. He handed one to Mr. Thomas. "Mr. Thomas, how long did you say you've been studying and researching here in the library?"

Mr. Thomas clinked glasses with Bart. "It'll be my four hundredth anniversary this Wednesday. I still remember how ecstatic I was to find it. All this knowledge in one place, incredible, and just for me."

Bart downed the wine in one gulp. "Just for you, aye? Well, let me tell you something. I'm going to do this thing I heard about. It's called a Web Tube. The normals down there, they make moving pictures, and they share 'em with each other on this here Web Tube. All the ancient colleges and secret societies, they're done for. All a curious soul need do is find the Web Tube. The Tube then carries the information to the student at her home. That's all. Crotchety old scholars not required. Gentlemen, the Craft is soon to be democratized.

Mr. Thomas, I suggest you invest in toadstools and spice worms. Ingredients are soon to be in high demand. I aim to teach craft work to them poor souls down there on a scale the world has never seen before. When I'm finished, there'll be no more struggles for food or energy, thermodynamics being what it is and all. They want water, they'll pull it from the air, just like you lot. It'll be all candy and nuts, and they'll all have a happy holiday."

Mr. Santana shook his head. "It's all been done before. You'll be laughed out of the intellectual community, or worse, burned at the stake. Look at what democracy did for Gaius Julius Caesar. I'll give you a hint. It didn't end well."

"I don't give a damn about the colleges, and no one's burning me at anything," Bart said. "You can be sure of that. This time, it'll be different. I have an inter-web."

33

A NEW BEGINNING

It had been a month since their ordeal in the park. Sammy thought they had been away long enough, and it was a perfect early autumn day for a long walk. He went to the park with a few friends but stepped away to check out the tunnel. "I'll be back in a few."

His eyes flittered back and forth. There was no sign of Bart or any cops. He hadn't seen Bart since that day and had hoped he would be there.

Elizabeth romped through the grass as usual. Sammy bent down and pulled a white tissue from her mouth. "No. I told you not to eat garbage from the ground. Yuck. Who knows where that's been?"

Elizabeth jumped, smiling.

"We're gonna go for a walk, and then we're going back home so I can do my chem lab experiments. Bob and Jane said we can go see June and Marmaduke after. He's a lot bigger than you, but he's nice, so don't be scared."

They passed the lampposts without a hitch.

"Tonight, we have Alex's party. She's valedictorian. It's kind of a big deal when a friend gets top grades in the whole school. She said you can come, but you have to be good. She just adopted a puppy around your age, so you'll have someone to play with."

Sammy stopped Elizabeth before entering the tunnel. He bent down and double-checked her sure-fit harness, making sure it was secure and she couldn't wiggle out. They walked into the tunnel. "Look, no doors, no steaks, and no cops, just the way we like it." Sammy rubbed the raised scar on his finger where the rune had burned into his skin. "It feels like it was all a dream. Did it even happen?"

Elizabeth snatched up some foreign object from the ground.

Sammy removed a small white ceramic shard from her mouth. "I told you, no eating trash." He put the piece of plate into his pocket. "Yeah. It happened."

THE END

Thank you for reading my book. It's been an honor
writing for you.

If you did or didn't enjoy this book, please feel free to send
your thoughts. I'd love to hear from you. You can contact me
via email at **mikejonesfiction@gmail.com**.

I hope you enjoyed the characters in The Magical Prison of
Middle Park. Some can also be found in these other titles in
my New Kent Series.

Chris Thurgood Saves the Future

Elizabeth Bennet: Shadow Hunter

The Fall of Port City

More information is available at my website.

mikejonesfiction.wordpress.com

Click here for updates from Mike Jones Fiction and receive a free copy of my next title.